Supernatural Hero

By Eran Gadot

Translated by Gilah Kahn-Hoffmann

Illustrated by Salit Krac

https://www.facebook.com/SupernaturalHero

Supernatural Hero

By Eran Gadot

Edited by Tsipi Sharoor

Translated by Gilah Kahn-Hoffman

Illustrated by Salit Krac

Production: Notssa

Table of Contents

Chapter One

Me, the Class Nerd

Of all the kids, I'm the only one who doesn't get invited to birthday parties. Or picked for a partner at school. Or sit with a bunch of friends at lunch. I've never been popular. I'm a nerd.

It's a good thing no one knows what goes on inside me.

When I'm alone, I cry.

Mom always asks me, "Andy, how was your day at school?"

"Everything's fine, "I usually answer. But I'm not sure she believes me. She knows that all the kids make fun of me because I'm really skinny, and I wear glasses, and I have this very white skin that turns bright red in the sun. I also have black hair and blue eyes like Grandpa. Oh, and I'm terrible at sports.

Mom's worried because she thinks I'm scared of everything and that I'm insecure. That's what she always whispers to Dad in the evening, when they're sitting and talking in the living room and they think I'm asleep. They also wonder if they should take me to a psychologist because I don't have any friends. I do have one friend – Tom –he's in the genius class.

I once had an imaginary friend named Victor. I talked to him about everything under the sun, even the most secret things. I also talk to Grandma, especially since she died. But I love my Grandpa more than anyone in the whole world. He's the only one who understands me.

Grandpa and I talk about almost everything, including stuff that adults don't usually discuss with kids. The only thing I haven't told him about is Zoe. I've overheard my big sister and her friends talking for hours about love at first sight. That's how I felt about Zoe. I met her last year in the fifth grade. she came to our school in the middle of the year, and in two minutes she was Queen of the Class. She has straight brown, shoulder-length hair and dimples, which make her smile the most beautiful one I've ever seen. She has big blue eyes, and when she laughs her teeth sparkle.

At recess, the boys play football and the girls sit on the benches, talking and watching the boys. Today, our class played against the other sixth grade class. Stuart scored two touchdowns and we beat them, two to one. All the other players jumped on Stuart and slapped him on the back. I saw how Zoe looked at him. I wish she would look at me like that. Then I cursed him inside and wished he would fall off his bike and break his leg, or that all the boys would give him the silent treatment, or that he would get sick, or that… in the end, I calmed down.

I haven't told anyone about the way I feel, not even Tom. We mostly talk about math. He has these wild ideas, and I'm the only one who listens to him. But the thing we like best is to play computer games. Tom is really good at all the new outer space games. He's passed all the levels and reached the moon.

At night, Mom always says to Dad, "I don't know what will become of that boy," but Dad always comes home worn out from working all day, and he doesn't have the energy for much beyond the TV news, so he's definitely not interested in me.

But somehow he finds the energy for my sister, Lynn. He even knows who her friends are and he knows what she's learning at school. He doesn't know anything about me. Grandpa knows everything about me. He always says that I'm an exceptional boy. If the kids in my class could hear how Grandpa talks about me, I know things would improve and they would invite me to their birthday parties.

"Think about good things and in the end they'll happen to you," Grandpa tells me."

So at recess I sit on the farthest bench in the schoolyard, talking to myself and thinking about good things. Suddenly I feel a bang on my head and I hear everyone laughing like crazy. They find the whack on my head very entertaining.

I look down so they can't see my face, but inside I'm furious and I'm cursing them. I leave the schoolyard and go to my classroom. They are so lucky they don't know what I wish I could do to them. If only a tiny bit of it could come true, they'd be finished.

Chapter Two

Mom

When I get home after school, Mom is already there. I can smell the hamburgers and chips she's cooking in the kitchen. I love it when she makes them for me. It's weird that she's here, though, because she never gets home before I do. Something special must have happened today.

Mom is in the middle of a long, involved telephone conversation with a woman from her office at the insurance company. They're talking about a big claim someone has against their company and she's saying that she isn't sure that the client is telling the truth. It seems that adults lie much more than kids do, but if I were to tell her that I can talk to grandma, she wouldn't believe me. She would be sure that I was making it up. And she would never have such a long conversation with me about it.

Finally she notices that I'm there.

"How was your day at school?" Her voice is kinder than usual.

Like always, I say it was fine.

"Are you sure that things are okay? Are the other kids playing with you?"

I'm so happy that she's interested I think I might burst. But before I can answer her, Lynn comes through the door with her friend. All of a Sudden two fifteen-and-a-half-year-old girls who think they're fashion models are standing in the kitchen.

"What are you doing home so early? Outta here! In your room!" Lynn screeches at me in her squeaky voice. She turns to her friend. "All he ever does is sit by himself and play on the computer, anyway."

"And all you ever think about is Facebook and chats," I say.

Lynn brings her face close to mine. "Outta here!"

Mom doesn't say anything.

When Lynn says something she's always right, because she's the big sister, and she's beautiful, and everyone always goes wild over her. She's in high school and she has loads of friends. She gets invited to all the birthday parties.

Grandpa is the only one who always says that I will be more successful than Lynn. "You'll see, she'll be asking you for help when you're older," he sometimes says. She can dream on. One of these days I'll be popular and they'll invite me to birthday parties and I'll have lots of friends, too.

I turn away and go to my room, but inside I'm cursing Lynn. If she could hear what I'm thinking she would never dare shout at me again. I slam my door. Lucky for me, Grandpa bought me a book of math puzzles. I can do five in five minutes.

I have the neatest room in the world. I have a blue bed that can turn into a couch, a grey cupboard, a desk with a computer and a giant screen, and even an executive chair that used to belong to Mom.Even with all that, all I do is sit and daydream about Zoe.

The Queen of the Class and the Class Nerd? Any chance that could work? Even in my imagination? It's a good thing mine is so overdeveloped.

Chapter Three

Lynn

Maybe it would be better if everyone hated me. At least they would be paying attention to me…

Tom's sick. He hasn't come to school for the past three days, and I'm going crazy at recess. I tried to talk to Stephen, but he didn't even pretend to listen to a word I said. David just walked past and body checked me. I fell and everyone laughed. My glasses got knocked off and it took me a few seconds to find them. The whole time their laughter was ringing in my ears.

Our schoolyard has one field for both football and basketball, so there are always fights: football or basketball? Usually the majority wants football, but once in a while they play basketball. Then the football players go and sit with the girls and also find time to harass Tom and me, the nerds. My class is on the third floor. The best thing is to sit and do math exercises until the bell rings. If Tom doesn't come to school tomorrow, I'm not coming either.

After school I go to visit Grandpa. We talk about the moon, the stars, the Big Dipper, and all sorts of fascinating things in the sky. Grandpa always tells me about them.

Sometimes we talk about money.

"You're excellent at math and that will help you to earn a lot of money. Then you'll be able to buy whatever you want," Grandpa says.

"Even friends?" I ask.

"Even friends." Grandpa laughs.

That gets me excited. I could have a giant birthday party and lots of people would come and I would give out presents.

Grandpa remembers how before the war, when he was a kid, his mother would always test his math.

"My mother would ask me to count shirts and socks and even to add up our bill at the grocery store."

"And did you get it right?" I ask.

"Not always, but I always said I knew the answer. Sometimes the grocer would tell me the answer."

I laugh. "So how did you learn?"

"My mother would ask me to calculate how many hours I spent with my friends, and how many hours I was at school. Then she would tell me to multiply and divide the numbers, until I started calculating everything all the time."

I start to calculate everything, too. For example, I work out how long it's been since I first set eyes on Zoe, how many times she's looked in my direction, and how many words she says in class.

"Grandma said you should make sure to get enough sleep," I say, fondly remembering my grandmother, who went to heaven a long time ago.

"She still takes care of me." Grandpa smiles. "I talk to her every night."

"What do you two talk about?"

"I'll tell you later, Andy." Grandpa yawns, and I can see he's really tired.

Grandpa has woken up every morning at 05:12, for the past eleven years, seventy-two days and seventeen hours, exactly.

On my way home I start working out how much that is in hours, minutes, and seconds.

Mom and Lynn are sitting in the kitchen, talking about the hunk in the other class who smiles at Lynn in the hallway at school. How much time can they spend talking about smiles at school? If I calculate the number of hours they sit and talk about the hunk, I'll get to several days, maybe even a week.

Mom doesn't acknowledge me, but Lynn sees me and screeches, "Go sit in your room, and don't poke your nose into other people's business!"

Again Mom doesn't say anything. She never sticks up for me – of course not, because Lynn's the eldest she gets everything she wants and she can treat me any way she likes. I don't say a word, but inside I curse her, and I hope that one day all the girls will freeze her out.

I go to my room and Grandma tries to calm me down. I don't take any notice of her, and start to work on the new book of math puzzles that Grandpa gave me. When I'm done with this one, he'll get me a new one for seventh graders. Even Tom doesn't understand the equations in those books. "I'll show them." Oops, I'm mumbling to myself again, it's a good thing no one can hear me. I want to get even better at math. Maybe one day Zoe will ask me a math question and I'll give her the answer faster than a computer could, faster than a fighter plane, and then, maybe, she'll…

Nooooo, she'll never go out with a nerd like me. No chance.

I think about Zoe all the time. If only she was my girlfriend. David's already had three girlfriends, Stuart has had two, and Mark has also had two. Everyone gets girlfriends, but I'm not everyone.

Mom opens my door. "Did you have a nice time at Grandpa's?" she asks. "And what would you like to eat?"

I want to tell her about Zoe, to let her know that I'm in love with a girl in my class. But I'm not sure if I'm allowed to talk about it like Lynn talks about the hunk. Maybe I'll talk to Dad about it at bedtime. If I could get a girlfriend, I mean Zoe, and if I could have friends, then Dad would be proud of me.

"Andy!" Mom calls me for the third time. "The food's ready; it's getting cold." She worries about food all the time. What terrible thing would happen to it if it got cold? I keep quiet. I'm afraid I'll make her angry, and then she'll tell Dad again that I drive her crazy and they should take me to a psychologist.

Chapter Four

Grandpa

On the way to school I notice a black cat walking toward me.

Grandma used to say that a black cat brings bad luck, and if you see one you have to knock on wood three times to protect yourself so nothing bad will happen to you. Grandpa would laugh and say that's nonsense. I actually think she might be right. So whenever I see a black cat, I knock three times on the first wooden thing I find. And in my heart, just like Grandma, I wish really hard that nothing bad will happen to me. On the way to school I pass a wooden electric pole and I knock on it three times and I even spit when no one's looking, because that's what Grandma says you should do to keep all the bad things away.

"Good for you, Andy!" she says.

But every time I asked Grandpa about it, he just said that it's a superstition, and then he would whisper in my ear that Grandma believed in all sorts of nonsense because of the war. Whenever anything doesn't make sense with Grandma and Grandpa it has something to do with the war.

I get to school twenty minutes before the bell and the class is empty. I sit and figure out how much time we have left until summer vacation – how many weeks, days, hours, minutes, and seconds. I'm concentrating so hard I don't notice that a few kids come into the class. Someone puts a paper bag over my head and then they start to hit me.

"He's talking to himself!" I hear David shout and everyone laughs.

The bell rings. I take the bag off my head. The boys are still laughing. I put my head down on my desk and I can't hold back my tears.

Then I hear a sweet voice, maybe the sweetest voice I've ever heard. "Is everything okay, Andy?"

Very slowly I lift my head and I see her. She has the deepest and most beautiful blue eyes in the whole world. She used my name! She actually knows my name! Yes! I shout, but silently, deep inside – luckily they can't hear how loudly I shout inside myself. My silent shout would probably shake the whole building. The main thing is that Zoe knows my name. Now I don't feel so bad.

The history teacher comes into the class and starts talking to us about World War II. I don't even hear what she's saying. All I can think about is Zoe's sweet voice saying my name. I wanted to answer her so much, but I couldn't speak. I'm drenched in a cold sweat. I imagine taking Zoe for a ride on the back of the bicycle I'm going to get one of these days. I imagine us riding to the mall, locking the bike outside, going up the escalator, holding hands, going to see a new 3D movie, buying a giant popcorn and sharing it.

I realize that the history teacher has been calling my name for awhile. Everyone's laughing.

"He's off in outer space!" Stuart shouts.

Someone throws a pencil that hits the tip of my ear. I look up at the teacher. She asks me to please repeat what she just said. But I haven't heard a word. My head is filled with the memory of Zoe's honey voice.

The history teacher sends me to the principal's office with a note that says one of my parents has to come to school to talk to her.

As I leave the class, out of the corner of my eye, I see Zoe, the only one who didn't laugh. She even made a face at David when he was laughing so loud you could hear him all the way down the hall. I go downstairs. The walls are covered with dirty handprints. I count 54 kids' handprints on the way to the principal's office. I stand around outside the office, looking at the photos of the graduating classes. I look for my sister's picture. I'm killing time, hoping the secretary might have to go out. But ultimately, I have to go in and give her the note, and she gives me a paper that says my mother should come to school the next day, after recess.

I don't know what to tell Mom. She'll be so angry. Now for sure she'll take me to therapy. Last time they took me I lost Victor, my imaginary friend. But maybe therapy would help me with Zoe… Maybe I'll get invited to birthday parties… I start to feel better. But what should I tell Mom?

I get home late and go straight to my room. There's no one there. Strange. Mom and Lynn should be home. I'm not really worried, but I don't like it. It doesn't feel right. When I phone Mom, she says she's at

Grandpa's and she'll be home later. What's she doing there? Normally she only visits him on the weekend. I decide to do some more equations in my math workbook. I'll probably finish the whole book before anyone comes home.

There are only a few pages left when I hear the door open. Mom and Lynn come in and just stand there. What's going on? I can tell by Mom's face that something has happened, but I don't ask any questions. Lynn is very quiet, which is really unusual for her. She goes straight to her room. I want to ask Mom if something has happened, but I feel as though I've lost my voice. I go back to my room and I can hear Mom whispering to Dad on the phone, but I can't make out what she's saying. Something is going on and I have no idea what it is. I start to feel afraid. Why isn't anyone telling me anything?

Mom comes into my room and says I should go to sleep early, that she has a headache and needs some peace and quiet. It's already late anyway. I eat a bowl of strawberries and get ready for bed. Then Dad comes home and I go to the living room. He hugs Mom tight, gives Lynn a kiss and pats me on the head. It feels so good. He never strokes my head when he comes home, but today he did.

I go back to my room and switch off the light, but I can't fall asleep. I hear Mom and Dad talking in the living room. I don't understand it all, but I manage to hear a few things.

"He's very sick. Cancer is serious," Mom says in a shaky voice.

Who are they talking about?

Mom cries softly and Dad says, "He's already eighty, and at least he lived long enough to know his grandchildren. He probably never believed he'd make it to eighty. It has been so hard for him, ever since Grandma died."

Obviously they're talking about Grandpa. I want to scream, but I can't make a sound. I start to shake. My Grandpa has cancer. Is it very bad? Will they let me see him? I want to hug him and Mom, too. I lie in my bed and I can't move. I hate cancer. Tomorrow I'll ask Tom a million questions. I'll go see Grandpa. I'll find a cure for him and he'll get better. Nothing will happen to him. I'll do everything for Grandpa.

Mom and Dad go to sleep but I can't sleep – I just toss and turn. I count to a thousand thirteen times. I have scary thoughts. I'm worried. It's two o'clock in the morning. I can't remember ever being awake at this hour before. I decide to go to Grandpa and stay with him.

Grandpa lives close by, just a five-minute walk. I've never left the house at this time. If Mom and Dad wake up, they'll be really mad at me and Mom will definitely take me to therapy. I decide to stay. Maybe I'll go visit Grandpa tomorrow, instead of going to school.

I never told Mom that she has to come to my school tomorrow. I couldn't talk to her. What would I say? At least Grandpa will be on my side. He will say to Mom, "Enough, leave him alone." She always listens to him.

I've got to go to sleep so tomorrow I'll be strong and I'll be able to help Grandpa. Mom seems so worried. It scares me. Even when Lynn had pneumonia and she stayed home from school for more than a week, Mom didn't look like that. Maybe it's really, really bad. I have to find a way to save Grandpa.

I have to.

Chapter Five

Dad

Dad wakes me and tells me to come have breakfast. I'm really frightened. They probably found out about what happened at school and now they're really mad at me.

I don't see Mom anywhere. Dad just sits at the table, points to the cereal and milk and says "Have some breakfast." Then he drinks his coffee and reads the morning paper.

There's a strong smell of coffee in the kitchen, like there always is when Dad makes coffee for himself. I sit at the table and I don't say a word. I don't feel hungry at all, because I'm so nervous. I'm sure they called from school.

Maybe it's a good sign that Dad's not saying anything, but now his silence is starting to get to me. Where's Mom? Why isn't she making my sandwich to take to school? Dad asks if I'm hungry and I say no. He goes back to his paper and then he looks at me and says, "Mom went to the hospital with Grandpa. I don't know when she'll be back, but I've taken the day off. I'll be here when you come home from school. Maybe we can do something together."

I am really surprised by what Dad said. He never has time for me. On the weekend he's always busy with his newspapers and his football games on TV. That's how he enjoys himself and I just sit in my room and play on my PlayStation. My body feels hot and I feel a surge of love for my dad. I want to tell him that the kids in my class are mean to me and sometimes they hit me. I'm also almost always alone at recess, and I'm in love with Zoe. I want more than anything to tell him. Maybe he would come with me to school, grab David, and tell him that if he ever touches me again he'll be really sorry. Then all the kids will know that from then on they had better not mess with Andy. My throat feels dry. I make a sandwich and shove it in my bag. Dad's staring at me with a serious look on his face.

"Is everything's okay?" he asks.

I nod my head and walk toward the door.

"I'll be here waiting for you when you come home; don't forget," Dad says.

On the way to school, I think about what I should say to the history teacher. If I say that Mom is in the hospital with Grandpa, maybe she'll forget about the whole thing. Maybe something good could come out of Grandpa being sick. That's stupid! I have to go and visit Grandpa. I

17

have to find a cure to make him better, fast, so in a split second he'll be healthy again. I've got to talk to Tom. His dad is a dentist, and Tom knows the names of at least a hundred and fifty diseases. For sure Tom will know which medicine Grandpa needs and how long it will take him to get better. I've got to find Tom.

I walk into my classroom. Zoe is already sitting there, talking to her best friend, Maya. They don't even see me come in. Still, I walk on tiptoes so they won't notice me. I put down my bag and go out to look Tom. I meet him coming to find me.

"Hi Tom, how are you feeling?" I ask him.

"Better," he says. "I had a slight flu."

"I really need your help," I say. "Grandpa is sick; he has cancer. You have to help me to find a cure."

Tom goes pale. He looks at me, but he doesn't say a word. This is really weird because he always has something to say. His reaction scares me and I feel like I'm suffocating. When the bell rings, I get my breath back.

"We'll talk at recess," he says and goes back to his classroom.

The teacher comes in and asks if my mother's coming after recess. I tell her that my mom is at the hospital with my grandpa and that he has cancer. The teacher looks at me with a horrified expression on her face. She tries to smile, but her smile is so false that the terrible feeling sweeping over me just gets worse.

"I wish you good health, Andy, and tell your mother as well. You can go in now."

I go in and sit down at my desk, next to Sally. I've been sitting next to her for more than three months, but we've never said a word to each other. Well, once we did. She said good morning and I nodded. I'd like to talk to her. Sally is one of the brainy kids, like me. She's thin and small and she has dark skin. She also wears big black glasses and has small black eyes, like a wolf. I'm sure Sally knows about cancer. Her mother is a head nurse at a hospital and during school vacations she always goes to work with her to help out with the patients. I know because at the beginning of the year she told the class what she did during the summer. But I don't dare ask her. I count the minutes. I can't wait for class to be over. At least today the teacher is leaving me alone. She probably feels sorry for me because of Grandpa, but she doesn't really know anything about what's wrong with him. She just knows it's cancer. I heard once that there are lots of kinds of cancer. Which kind does Grandpa have? I pray that he has the easiest kind, that he can take the strongest pills and get better fast. I have to go visit him. No one tells me anything and I don't know what's going on.

The bell interrupts my thoughts and I hurry to Tom's class. He's already waiting for me outside the door, and we walk to the farthest bench in the schoolyard, where no one else is sitting.

"Tom, I have to know everything about cancer. I have to help my grandpa," I'm practically shouting.

Tom tells me that there are many different kinds of cancer and that it's a very serious illness, but that you can get better. It depends on a few things, like when they discover it and what type of cancer it is. I don't know what to say. I understand that there are some types of cancer you can recover from, and some that are really dangerous, and you can even die from them. When Tom explains it to me it's pretty easy to understand. But it's still scary. I don't know what to think. What if Grandpa has the worst kind?

"He could die of it," says Tom. He explains that the stronger a person's body is, the better the chance of winning.

19

I don't understand why Tom is talking about a disease like it's a sports competition. What's all this about "winning"? People just have to take medicine and get better. I don't feel like talking to Tom about it anymore because all that matters now is that Grandpa gets better and… wins.

I go home. Dad opens the door and smiles when I come in. He asks if I want to do something together. I don't know what we could do, but then I think it would make him happy if we play a soccer game on the PlayStation, so I suggest that. I know he likes Barcelona, so I choose that team for him. I choose Chelsea for myself because I think the name is funny. I don't know whether it's a good team, but from the look on Dad's face, I can tell that he knows the team and he's glad. He asks me if I know the team and I'm too embarrassed to tell the truth, so I say yes. I can fake it because I know the names from the PlayStation game. So I manage to make Dad a little happy. It was worth the lie. How often have I managed to make my dad happy? I'm not like David or Stephen who go to games with their fathers all the time. I've never been to a real game; sports don't interest me one bit.

Dad actually has pretty good skills, but I still beat him four to three. Tom and I play a lot so I know what I'm doing. Dad wants to play again. I feel so close to him and really good about myself. I want to tell him that I'm in love with Zoe and to get his advice about asking her to be my girlfriend. Dad had lots of girlfriends. Mom told me once that all the girls wanted him, but she was the one who conquered him. "Conquered him" – like he was a fortress defended by dragons in Harry Potter world. But I don't manage to say a word. I feel safe and relaxed, and it's enough that Dad and I are together.

I win the second game as well. This time it's a lot easier, because Dad's getting tired. If you're not used to playing, it's hard. But Dad doesn't like to lose and he starts to get irritated. I decide to let him beat me next time. I prefer a happy Dad, so I lose the third game, one to two.

Dad lifts his hands in a victory salute and wants to play again, but just then Mom comes in. She's back from the hospital. She doesn't say anything, but her face really scares me. She makes a gesture with her hand that Dad should follow her, and motions to me to stay put. Dad goes to the living room and I fill up with fear. Please, just don't let anything happen to Grandpa.

Chapter Six

Grandma

Grandma died when I was really little, and other than her, I never met anyone who died or was in danger of dying. Mom and Dad don't tell me anything. They think I'm a little kid. They try to hide Grandpa's illness from me, but I need to know how he is. I see Mom's face and she looks so worried. I know my mom, and I've never seen her like this. I want to talk to her. I want to go to Grandpa. I can't wait anymore. I walk out of my room. It's 05:55 in the evening. Mom and Dad are sitting at the kitchen table. Dad's drinking coffee and eating cookies. They don't notice that I left my room. I stand near the bathroom, but I can't hear Mom that clearly.

She's saying she talked to the doctor. She asked what stage cancer he has. I don't understand what she's talking about, but I hear her say "Stage Four, advanced." To me that sounds like the name of a new PlayStation game.

"Do they think there's any point in operating? How much time does he have left?" Dad asks.

I freeze in place. I gasp and I start to shake.

"His prognosis is two months, sixty days." Mom starts to cry and I try to understand what I've just heard.

Grandpa has sixty more days to live. My beloved Grandpa is going to die and the doctor says there's nothing to be done. I can't accept it. What's a doctor's "prognosis" anyway? It sounds like the name of an ancient sword from the new Sin City. I mean, Grandpa always says that anything's possible. He always tells me about how he saw death up close a few times in the war, but always, at the last minute, he was saved. There has to be a solution; I have to find something.

I go into my room. I can't stand to hear Mom cry. I call Tom. He's playing chess on the computer. I ask him to stop playing and help me find a cure for Grandpa. I tell him everything I've heard, and I ask him to do a Google search for the answers. Tom promises to do the research and get back to me. I'm sure he'll find something. He knows so many things that other people don't know; that even adults don't know. I count almost twenty minutes. I call Tom again and he answers right away. He tells me that he's found a clinic in Mexico City that treats terminally ill patients and that they can save Grandpa.

"Terminally ill?" I repeat.

Tom explains that that's what you call people who are going to die soon. No one ever talks to me about death. Kids don't usually talk about stuff like that, but I can talk to Tom about anything – even the most grown-up things in the world.

"They have all sorts of treatments. There are even stories about patients who were told they only had a week to live, and then they were saved."

I am so happy that I might be able to save Grandpa. I have to talk to Mom about this. Mom would do anything for Grandpa. She always tells me that she loves him so much and how he was always on her side when she was a kid. I ask Tom to print out everything he finds and bring it to school for me tomorrow.

I go to the kitchen and find Dad sitting there with Lynn. They're talking about a music reality show. Who cares? Grandpa is about to die!!! I shout inside. I ask where Mom is.

and "She went to bed. She's very tired," Dad answers. "What would you like to eat?"

I'm not hungry. I want to tell Mom that I have an idea that can save Grandpa. I think about telling Dad, but in the end I decide it's better not to. I don't feel like dealing with Lynn butting in. She only cares about herself and her friends, anyway. I take an apple from the fridge, cut it in half, and go into the living room. I hear Lynn describing the singer who made it to the finals, and Dad saying he thought the blind girl had a better chance of winning. I think it would even be okay if Grandpa goes blind, just so long as he doesn't die. I can't think straight. Grandpa has less than sixty days left to live – that's what the doctor told Mom. I've got to do something. I'll go to sleep early. I have to be strong tomorrow. I go back to the kitchen and ask, "How far is it to Mexico?"

Dad looks at me in surprise. "Why are you interested in Mexico all of a sudden?"

It takes me a couple of seconds, and then I tell him that I have a geography project. He thinks for a minute then says it's quite a long flight – about ten hours. That sounds like a lot to me. I've never been on a plane. I bet it's really scary. But I'd do anything to save Grandpa, even if it really scares me. I'm ready to fly with him and stay with him in Mexico City until he gets better. I don't care how long it takes. I don't have anyone here except for Tom, anyway, and I can always Skype with him. Sometimes, when I'm home alone, I Skype with him from Lynn's computer. She has a camera and a microphone, but when she's home she doesn't let me touch her computer.

Mom will be so happy that we've found a way to save Grandpa. She'll think I'm a hero. I am a hero! I go into my room and start pulling clothes out of the closet. I don't know what the weather's like in Mexico, so I take out long sleeved and short sleeved shirts, pants and shorts. I get into bed but I can't sleep. I'm scared Grandpa will die. I don't even know what happens to people when they die. I have to talk to Grandpa; he'll explain everything. We always talk like two grownups. Once he told me how in the war a few people died right next to him, but he managed to get away. He even tried to save someone, but in the end that person died, too. I remember I asked him where the dead people go, and Grandpa looked up at the ceiling and said they go to heaven. I didn't ask anything else, but now I need to know. Probably none of the kids know anything about death. Maybe Tom knows.

There have to be cures for every kind of sickness; you just have to look for them. I better get some sleep and in the morning I'll tell Mom. She'll be happy and I'll fly with them to Mexico City. Grandpa will get the special medicine and then we'll come back home. While we're there I'll have time to think about Zoe, and when we get back I'll ask her if she wants to be my girlfriend. I'll ask Grandpa for advice. He always has great advice and he tells me exactly what to do and how to do it. I just have to think of the right questions.

Grandpa used to work as an accountant at the supermarket, adding and subtracting and calculating how many things were bought and sold and how much the workers should be paid. When I was little, during summer vacations I would go to work with him. He would give me paper and I would draw dragons and crazy imaginary animals. Grandpa would stick my pictures on his wall and give me a candy for each picture he hung up. Then he'd ask me to count the candies he gave me. I would have to count all the pictures hanging on the wall, and when I got the number right, he would smile and put another candy in my pocket, and another one in my hand for Lynn. I always wanted it to be summertime so I could go to work with Grandpa.

But Grandpa stopped working after Grandma died. She had a disease that she caught in the war. Grandpa tells me she's waiting for him to join her in heaven.

"But Grandma told me that she's not in a hurry for you to come," I remind him. He just smiles and says that it will be many years yet. I really hope he's right.

Grandma died when I started first grade and now I'm in sixth grade. Lately, Grandma and I talk a lot. She's still waiting for Grandpa. I wonder what she does up there. Maybe Grandpa knows. I want answers. I have to let Grandma know that there's no chance of Grandpa joining her yet. He has to stay with us until I'm Zoe's boyfriend, until I finish high school. Grandpa will buy me a little car and we'll go on fishing trips together. We'll stay up all night fishing for big fish, and he'll tell me all about the war and how he escaped death so many times. He'll tell me how he married Grandma, and then Uncle Eric was born, and five years later Mom was born.

Grandpa has two kids. There's Eric, Mom's brother, who's a lawyer with a big office where he has lots of workers. He always wears a suit and tie, even in the hottest weather. I once asked him how he could dress like that when it's really hot outside, and he said a man in his position has an image to keep up. What kind of position makes you have to sweat and suffer in the heat when you could wear summer clothes and feel cooler? I didn't understand what he was talking about, but I decided that I don't want a position like that, if it means I'll have to sweat all day. I want a different kind of position that comes with shorts and sandals.

I look at my watch and see the time is 10:22 p.m. I'd better get some sleep.

Chapter Seven

Mexico City

I wake up in the morning feeling sure that I will save Grandpa. I can't wait for Mom to wake up so I can tell her about the place in Mexico City where they cure people who have cancer. We'll fly there together and stay with Grandpa until he gets better. I'm sure Mom will be so happy. Yesterday she told Dad that she would do anything to save Grandpa. I want to be Mom's hero and Grandpa's, too. I pace in my room, but quietly, so I won't wake Lynn. So she won't start screaming at me.

I hear footsteps in the living room. They sound like they're coming toward my room. It's six in the morning. In my house everyone wakes up at seven. The footsteps come closer. I freeze. I can hardly breathe. Now they seem to stop right outside my door and I can hear someone breathing hard. I jump into bed and pull the covers over my head. When I peek from under the covers I see my doorknob slowly turning. Who can it be? I hide my head again. I hear the door opening. Footsteps in my room. I peek again and I see Mom. She sits beside me and hugs me.

"What's wrong, Andy?" she whispers. I burst into tears and hug her so tightly. She strokes my head and tries to calm me.

"Don't worry, sweetheart, I'm here. Everything's okay." She keeps stroking my head and she kisses my forehead. "I love you, Andy."

"Mom, I heard footsteps in the living room and I was so scared. I was afraid that someone had broken into our house."

Mom keeps hugging and kissing me. "Go back to sleep now. I also couldn't sleep," she says.

"Because of Grandpa?"

"I'm very worried about him."

I look at Mom's face and she looks just like an angel. I love her so much.

"I can help Grandpa," I blurt out.

Mom's eyebrows rise. "Help? What do you mean? Grandpa's sick."

"I know. Grandpa has cancer."

Mom looks straight into my eyes. "Who told you?"

"I heard you talking to Dad."

"Andy, don't even think about it. Uncle Eric and I will do everything we can to help Grandpa, everything!"

"But Mom," I say with confidence, "I have a cure for Grandpa. I can save him."

She tries to smile. "My sweetie pie, I really appreciate how much you want to save Grandpa, but this is a horrible illness and you can't always save the person who has it. We are in contact with the top doctors and we're all working together to do the best we can for Grandpa."

"I found a place where they can cure him. They've already saved lots of people who had cancer, even terminally ill people. They can cure Grandpa, too!"

"What are you talking about, my sweetheart? I'm in touch with all the best doctors."

"I don't mean here; I mean far away."

Mom looks at me, confused. "Where?"

"Promise me that if you go there with Grandpa, you'll take me with you. Promise me!"

Mom smiles a wide smile and I feel calmer. Sometimes moms are the best thing in the world. I want to hug her and hug her and tell her about Zoe, but now the most important thing is to save Grandpa. Mom sits and strokes my hair.

"I found a special hospital in Mexico City that saves lots of people who have cancer."

She looks very surprised. "Mexico City?" she almost shouts.

It's 06:34 in the morning. I'm worried that Lynn will wake up. I don't want her to barge into my room and bug me when I'm with Mom.

"What are you talking about? Why are you talking about Mexico City? It's very far from here."

"Tom checked for me on the Internet. He did research to find out where you can save people with cancer and he also read lots of stories about people who were saved. Grandpa always says that anything is possible, and I'm sure that it's possible to save him. We can save him. I've even packed my clothes for the trip – but we have to check what the weather's like there. Tom will bring all the information to school today and then we can fly: me, you, and Grandpa. I'll help you and Grandpa, and we'll come back home when Grandpa gets better. We can win."

I can't believe how I'm talking, as if I'm so sure of myself. I never had such a grown-up conversation with Mom. It's the first time that Mom and I ever sat and talked like this, like she talks with Lynn. Mom's staring at me and really paying attention to me. But when she starts to talk, I realize she isn't going to follow my plan.

"Andy, I don't think you understand. We are in contact with the best doctors there are. Medicine is very advanced here. I'm sure they have great doctors in Mexico City, but I don't think that's the solution for Grandpa. Never mind all that now. Just go and visit Grandpa today. Spend some time with him. He really misses you and it will make him feel better to see you. Leave the medical treatment to Uncle Eric and me. We are checking every possibility."

"But Mom, lots of cancer patients have already been saved by the doctors in Mexico City. People wrote on the Internet that they were really about to die and they only had a few days to live and in Mexico City they were saved. We mustn't give up. Mom, we have to save Grandpa."

"Andy, sweetheart, do me a favor; I'm having a very hard time with Grandpa's illness, leave this to me."

I swallow past the lump in my throat. "At least read what Tom brings me. Maybe there really is a cure there for Grandpa."

"Andy, please, I'm asking you to forget about this. Just go and visit Grandpa after school."

"Even Grandma told me we should try," I blurt.

"Enough, stop talking about Grandma. She died a long time ago." Mom gives me a kiss on the forehead and gets up.

"But Mom—"

"Get ready for school." She cuts me off. "And stop sleeping with your socks on all night, you'll get eczema. It's a skin disease that gets passed on from generation to generation in our family."

I feel like I'm about to drown in tears of frustration. Why won't Mom let me save Grandpa? She won't even read the information that Tom found. I can't sit and do nothing! I have to go and talk to Grandpa. He's the one who's sick and no one else can decide for him what he should do. I have to get all the printouts about Mexico City from Tom and take them to Grandpa and convince him. Grandpa's not afraid of anything. He's been right up close to death a few times, and he always managed to survive. I'll show Mom – they'll cure him and I'll be her hero.

It's after seven now. I can hear Mom and Lynn talking. Dad says kids shouldn't have to worry about diseases; they should think about good things, like sports. There he goes again with his football, as if the game isn't some kind of mental disorder, with a bunch of lunatics chasing a stupid ball and jumping all over each other like nutcases when someone manages to kick it into a net or put it down over a line. When it comes to Dad, all good things have something to do with a ball.

I can't think of anything other than Grandpa. I go to the kitchen and say good morning to Dad and Lynn. Dad offers me toast and jelly but I don't want food. I only want to meet Tom and get the information about Mexico City.

Lynn looks at me and screeches, "Can't you fix your hair so you won't look like such a nerdy geeky loser."

I wonder why she only used three insults. I don't bother to answer her, but inside I'm burning up. Lucky for her I keep everything inside. If she could feel the heat in me, she'd get a burn that would scar her for the rest of her life. It's none of her business how I wear my hair. She always has a comment to make. Even Grandma says that Lynn's annoying.

Chapter Eight

Self Confidence

They always tell kids that when someone dies they go to heaven. But what happens next? We have to fill in the missing parts by ourselves, and everyone's imagination goes off in a different direction. It reminds me of the Tooth Fairy. My mom was always the fairy who waited until I fell asleep so she could slip a present under my pillow. But she never told me that *she* was really the Tooth Fairy. One night, after my tooth fell out and I went to bed, I couldn't sleep. Mom tiptoed into my room and put a toy watch under my pillow. That's when I realized that the Tooth Fairy doesn't exist and all those years she was just making up a story that sounded really good to a little kid when his baby teeth started to fall out.

This time it's a different story—Grandpa's story—and I feel like Mom either doesn't really want to tell me the story, or that she doesn't know how to make me part of it. I decide to skip school today and go see Grandpa. I've never skipped school before.It's not really a nerdy thing to do, but I feel that I have to talk to Grandpa right away.

I walk to Grandpa's house and knock twice on the door. I can hear him walking slowly, stopping to look through the peephole, and then he opens the door.

"What are you doing here, Andy?" Grandpa is half-scolding, half-smiling.

"I missed you and I had to come and talk to you."

"Your mother will be angry, but I'll talk to her."

I go in and sit in the living room. Grandpa sits down beside me and I examine him closely, checking for signs of cancer. I can't see anything different about him; maybe he's better already? Grandpa stares back at me.

"What are you looking for?" he asks.

"Cancer," I say. "I can't see any sign of it."

Grandpa smiles. "There aren't any signs, my boy. It's all inside, you can't see anything."

"So maybe it went away?" I ask hopefully.

Grandpa shakes his head. "Andy, cancer is a tough disease that attacks from within. It starts in one specific place in the body. In my case, it's the liver, and it slowly spreads to other organs. The cells in the body are destroyed. Sometimes there are treatments called chemotherapy or radiation that can help you beat the disease, but sometimes it's too late, or the treatment doesn't work, and in the end the person dies."

"I'm sure there's something we can do! My friend Tom looked on the Internet and he found out about this place in Mexico City where terminally ill patients got better and were saved from dying."

"That's not for me, my boy. I'm too old. It seems my time has come. Grandma has already been waiting for me up there for too long. I talked to her yesterday and I promised her that I'll be there soon." I start to shake all over and Grandpa hugs me. "It's the way of the world, old people have to die."

"But Grandpa, I don't want you to leave me." I start to cry. " I love you."

Grandpa pats my head. "I'm not planning to leave you forever. I'll watch over you from on high, and I'll be with you every step you take."

"Really?" I look closely at Grandpa, searching for some kind of hope in what I'm hearing. "I don't understand how you can watch out for me if you're dead."

"Listen Andy." Grandpa takes a deep breath. "Some people come back as ghosts—those are the ones who have unfinished business."

"And you'll come back?"

"I promised to help you, so that's my obligation. Life isn't over when you die; the spirit lives on."

I'm not sure what he means when he says the spirit lives on.

I look into Grandpa's big blue eyes. They look just like Zoe's eyes. Like you could dive into them and feel the waves washing over you. And Grandpa has this great-sounding voice so that when he tells you a story it's relaxing to listen and you pay attention to every word. He loves to tell stories and I love to listen to them. Then I ask him lots of questions when he's finished. He answers every one of my questions and always reminds me that the most important thing is to know what to ask. Grandpa talks to me like he would talk to a grownup; he never makes me feel like a little kid and he never avoids the tough questions.

"Will I be able to see you?"

"It's okay, Andy. I'll try to explain it better. What is your life, your body, your soul? Your soul is the part of you that exists with and beyond your body. But the minute your body stops functioning, your soul simply leaves it and goes on to live forever, without a body."

"How can you live without a body? I mean you can't run or jump or play on the PlayStation or hold hands with your girlfriend."

Grandpa grins at me. "This is the first time I've heard you mention a girlfriend."

"I wanted to talk to you about her."

"Is there a girl you like?"

37

I feel myself turning red and Grandpa gets it right away. "Tell me about her, Andy. What's her name?"

"I haven't told anyone about her," I say.

"It's okay." Grandpa takes my hand. "I'll help you."

"Her name is Zoe and she's in my class. I think I love her." I feel myself blushing again. "But I'm too shy to talk to her. She's the prettiest girl in the class, so I don't stand a chance."

Grandpa gives me a hug. "Never think like that, Andy, and remember something important: Everything is possible. You just have to believe in yourself. It all depends on you."

"So you can get better?"

"No," Grandpa replies. "There are some things that don't depend on you, but on medical science, on drugs, on a person's age and a whole lot of other things that don't always make up the prettiest picture. But I promise you that if you want Zoe to be your girlfriend, she will be."

I'm so excited and I imagine myself talking to Zoe at recess, asking her if she wants to be my girlfriend. She smiles and says yes, and that she's been waiting for me to ask her. We hold hands and walk out to the schoolyard together and everyone comes up to us to say congratulations. Even David whispers in my ear, "Nice going. The prettiest girl in the class chose you!" And all the kids are looking at me and I can tell that they're all jealous and they wish they were me... but then Grandpa sneezes hard and I come back to earth.

"I'll help you, I promise," Grandpa says. "If that's what you really want, you and Zoe will be boyfriend and girlfriend."

"It'll never work," I say. "Everyone is after her. Neil bounces his ball right next to her, David shows off on his skateboard, Stuart writes funny poems to her, and *I've* never even said one word to her."

I can tell Grandpa anything.

"Ask her to tell you her favorite color," Grandpa says.

"Why?" I wonder.

"After that, every time she sees the color she likes best, she'll think of you. You have to start talking to her about the things she likes and those things will start to connect the two of you."

"I'm sure we don't like the same color."

"But you can tell her that your mother likes the color purple and you'll see it's her favorite, too."

"How do you know that she likes purple?" I ask.

"The pretty ones always like purple. Believe me, I've checked."

Grandpa always knows what to say, I love to talk to him so much. My throat closes up as I remember Mom on the phone with the doctor, and Grandpa notices I'm shaking again.

"Andy, are you okay?" he asks.

I can't look him in the eye. "Mom says you only have fifty-nine days left to live."

Grandpa answers me simply, "That's what the doctors say. I've already packed up my stuff. I'm ready to die. I'm eighty years old. I grew up in Romania, fled to Russia when the war broke out, and escaped death a few times before I made it to this country. I fought in two wars and I've had happy times and I've had hard times. I've laughed and cried and sang and danced and loved and been happy and sad. I don't regret even one moment. I always tried to do the best I could. Remember – if you give your all, even if you don't get exactly what you want, you still win."

I feel so close to Grandpa. He talks to me like I'm grown up and he doesn't hide anything from me.

"They always told me that I'm a good man, even too good." He chuckles. "Remember that goodness isn't weakness. The good guys beat the bad guys in the end. The most important thing is to be a decent person." Grandpa's getting tired and his eyes are starting to close. He's talking slowly and softly. "Andy, I have always believed in you. You'll go far."

I feel strong and confident. I could ask Zoe to be my girlfriend right now, stand up to David, look straight into his eyes and tell him that from now on he'd better leave me alone. I could beat Stuart in a race and play Neil one-on-one in basketball. Grandpa makes me feel strong and secure and I start to believe in myself.

I get a big hug and a kiss from Grandpa and I give him one too. Then he goes to his room to lie down. I let myself out. I feel good. It's 12:35. I'll go to Tom's house and wait for him to come home from school. I want to tell him about Zoe and play on the PlayStation with him.

I don't know what to do about getting today's homework. Maybe I'll ask Sally. We've been sitting next to each other for such a long time and she's pretty nerdy herself. She'll probably be happy if I call her. I'll catch up on my school work at Tom's house and then I'll go home. Anyway, I'm sure no one noticed that I didn't come to school. No one cares about the class nerd. But I'm not going to stay a nerd. I'm going to be Zoe's boyfriend. I'll show all the geeks that one of us can go out with the Queen of the Class. All you have to do is think like a King.

Chapter Nine

Tom

Tom breaks the Oreo-eating record hands-down. I've never seen anyone eat so many of those cookies. When he opens the door I burst out laughing because he has dark Oreo crumbs and white cream all over his face. He didn't even notice.

No one's home at Tom's and he's watching the science channel, a program about brain research. He has room in his head for all the most interesting things. He thinks about them and examines them from every angle until he understands them. He is the most curious kid I've ever met. I also like to research things. I researched all the different kinds of bicycles that are good for kids, because Mom promised me a new bike after we get our report cards in the middle of the year. Since then I've been checking on the Internet and I think I've found the one I want. I asked Tom to check for me too and he found a bike in Canada that is really light and super fast. But who wants a bike like that? I want the best-looking bike, better than the one that Stuart has and faster than the one that David has; a bike that is also good for taking another person on the back. I already dream about taking Zoe on the back of my bike. Together we'll go for a ride, even to the mall to see a movie, and one day we'll ride to the park and I'll only bring her home after it gets dark.

Tom has to call my name three times before I realize I'm daydreaming.

"These days you're always off somewhere, dreaming," Tom says.

"Grandpa says that if you don't dream, your dreams can't come true, so that means that if someone dreams, he's going to make them happen," I say.

Tom smiles. He likes the things Grandpa tells me. He always says that my grandpa is a very wise man.

"How's your grandfather?" he asks.

"He already told my grandma that he'll be with her soon."

"You're not going to Mexico City?"

"He and my mom decided that he should get treatment here, even though the doctors give him only fifty-nine days to live."

"Since when do doctors tell people when they're going to die? A doctor is supposed help a patient stay alive, not to tell him that his time's up. No one can know that for sure, it's just an estimate."

"But it looks like things really are pretty bad," I say. "Grandpa realized that it's the end and he won't let anyone move him from here, certainly not to Mexico City."

"We should be doing kid stuff," Tom announces. "Let's play on the PlayStation."

Last vacation, Tom and his family went to London for a week. Ever since they came back he's been practicing an English accent. He's crazy about some new PlayStation game he got there, that they don't sell here. I've never been on a trip outside the country. Tom pulls me into the game. I wanted to call Sally and find out what I missed today, but it's easy to forget about that.

The time flies by and I notice it's dark outside. Tom's mom comes into the room and says "Hi."

Tom says hi back without even turning around and keeps on playing.

""It's late," his mom announces. "You should be getting home now, Andy."

I check my watch and see it's two minutes to seven – I have to move! Mom will be angry. She doesn't even know that I skipped school today. I get my stuff together. Tom's still playing. He can play for three days without noticing what's going on around him. He's always breaking new records, while all I do is dream about taking Zoe on the back of my bike, and of our being boyfriend and girlfriend, and of me not being the class nerd anymore, and everyone wanting to be my friend. Tom never worries about stuff like that. To him, the newest 3D game is the coolest thing in the world. Tom told me that Bill Gates, one of the richest men in the world, is a nerd like we are and everyone wants to be like him, rich and successful. So what? Does he mean that it's worth it to stay a nerd?

Chapter Ten

59 Days

On the way home I think about Grandpa.

He'll leave me soon. He's going to die. It can't be.

When I get home Mom's talking on the phone. I slip past her and go to my room. Through the wall I can hear the voices of Lynn and her friends. They're probably talking about the hunks in their class. I really couldn't care less what they're talking about. I put my bag on the floor and throw myself on my bed. I can hear Mom asking for the head of the department at the hospital and I start to sweat. From her voice I can tell things are really bad and I'm afraid something has already happened to Grandpa, but I don't dare go and ask her. She finishes the call and then she goes into the living room. I run to her and she tries to smile at me, but she looks really bad.

"What happened?" I ask.

"They've put Grandpa in the hospital," she says.

I start shaking again. How can it be? I saw him just a few hours ago and if the doctor is right, he still has fifty-nine days. I remember that Tom said it's only an estimate and no one really knows exactly how many days anyone has left.

Mom has her handbag and her keys and she's standing by the door. "Tell Dad I've gone to the hospital."

I want to tell her to take me with her, so I can help look after Grandpa, but I can't speak. My throat closes up and I can't make a sound. I'm so bad in situations when I have to act fast. Mom closes the door behind her. My eyes fill with tears as I think about the worst thing that can happen. I can't stop thinking about it. Will Grandpa really die? I should have gone with Mom to the hospital. I can't just sit here alone, not knowing what's happening with Grandpa. I'm more afraid than I've ever felt in my life. I want to phone Mom but I can't move.

Lynn passes me on her way to the kitchen, grabs a bag of chips from the cupboard, and turns to go back to her room. When she sees me she yells, "What are you looking at? Get into your room!"

I feel like I'm burning up. This time I can't take it from her. I look at her and I scream like I've never screamed in my life, "Shut your ugly trap and get into your room before I kill you!"

Lynn freezes on the spot. I've never shouted at her before. I always lower my head when she insults me, but this time I feel like I've finally had enough. I can't let her do it anymore. I'm not her punching bag. I can hardly believe what I just did, though.

Lynn is in shock. She goes to her room without saying another word.

I feel strong and powerful. I finally put her in her place. Thanks, Grandpa, for making me strong, I whisper. I go to my room but I can't calm down. A few minutes pass and I hear a knock at my door. Lynn's standing there staring at me with frightened eyes. I've never seen her like that.

"What do you want?" I ask.

"Do you know that Grandpa's in the hospital?"

"I know," I say. "He has fifty-nine days left to live."

Lynn cries softly. It's the first time I've seen her thinking about someone other than herself.

"Mom says he'll get better," she says.

"I'm sure he will," I say. "Don't worry."

She goes back to her room and I close my door and phone Mom, but she doesn't pick up. That scares me again. I think about going to the hospital by myself, but I'm scared Mom will be angry at me. Another knock at the door makes me jump a foot in the air.

Lynn's standing there again with a notebook in her hand. "Listen, can you help me with my math homework?"

We've just had a big fight and now she's asking me for help? Even though that makes me really mad I decide to do it. I solve the two equations for her. So long as she doesn't think she can count on me in emergencies, because every day is an emergency of some kind for her.

Lynn glances at my garbage can and notices all the pages that I crumpled up and threw away. "Draw a heart or a smiley, that always does the trick," she says and she smiles. I feel I'm turning as red as a tomato. We've never talked about things like that.

I hear Dad coming in and I run to him.

"Mom's at the hospital," I tell him.

"I know."

"How's Grandpa?"

"Not good."

"What's 'not good'?"

"I don't know, Andy, Mom's supposed to call me."

I go back to my room. Mom doesn't call. Scary movies are playing in my head. I feel like I'm going insane.

"Good night," says Dad.

The time is 10:48. It's late at night. Mom still hasn't called and I can't take it. My heart is pounding so hard. I have to find out what's going on with Grandpa. I guess Dad hears me pacing and he comes into my room.

"Try to go to sleep, sweetheart," he says.

"I have to know what's happening with Grandpa."

Dad tells me that Mom is with him, and he'll fill me in when I wake up in the morning.

As if I could fall asleep now. I realize that I haven't thought about Zoe for hours – I've only thought about Grandpa. He promised to stay with me and watch over me at least until I'm Zoe's boyfriend. It's already after 11:00 and my eyes keep closing. Pretty soon I fall into a deep sleep. I see a tiny dot of white light far away that seems to be calling to me, but every time I take a step toward it, it moves a step way. I feel as though I'm in its power. I close my eyes, but I can't get away from the light that has come right up to me and is now flashing in my face. I can feel it. And then I'm terribly hot. The heat seems to strangle me so I can hardly breathe, and I feel like something very powerful is happening. My whole body hurts. I open my eyes. I'm lying on my bed and I can't move a muscle. I don't want to call Dad because I don't want him to worry. Deep inside I feel that something important is happening to me. I think it's what Mom calls intuition.

Or maybe it's just a stomachache or an anxiety attack.

Chapter Eleven

Grandpa Goes to Heaven

I hear Mom crying and Dad talking on the phone. The time is nearly 08:00 a.m. but Mom hasn't come to wake me up. I lie in bed, afraid to move. I hear her crying getting louder and stronger and I start to cry, too. I know something terrible has happened to Grandpa. Dad is talking about the cemetery. I feel myself going numb again and I can't move. I hear Lynn's door and her footsteps and I manage to get up and follow her to the living room.

Mom sees us and through her tears she says, "Lynn, Andy, Grandpa passed away."

My throat closes up again. I lose my voice. I feel panicked and scared. I want to die. "Grandpa's dead, Grandpa's dead, Grandpa's dead!" I shout inside, without making a sound. I get the shakes again and my heart beats like a heavy motorcycle in sixth gear. Lynn hugs Mom.

Dad finishes his phone call and says, "The funeral is today at 3 o'clock. We have to let people know. What about Andy?"

"You don't take children to the cemetery," Mom says.

To my surprise, Dad insists. "He was very close to Grandpa. He should be there."

And Lynn says, "Leave him alone, Dad, it will only give him nightmares."

I hope she really means it and she's not making fun of me. Anyway, at the moment my biggest nightmares are her friends. I have to speak up and tell Mom that I'm coming; there's no way Grandpa is leaving without me. I have to say goodbye. I'm crying enough tears to fill a swimming pool. I go to Mom and hug her harder than I've ever hugged her before.

"He loved you so much," she whispers to me.

"And I loved him more than anything in the world. He was my best friend." I give her a piercing look. She moves away from me and goes into the kitchen.

"I'm coming to the funeral!" I shout. Mom opens her mouth to say something, but before she can speak I cry, "I don't care what anyone says, I need to say goodbye to Grandpa." I fling myself on the carpet, screaming and crying. "Grandpa's dead. Grandpa's dead. My Grandpa is dead!"

Chapter Twelve

Grandpa Comes Down from Heaven

Mom is wearing black clothes, big sunglasses and a big black hat. Dad's wearing jeans and a black shirt, and Lynn is wearing a black dress and sunglasses. I'm wearing the blue tracksuit that Grandpa gave me and a blue shirt with a small symbol of a horse. Mom keeps trying to dry her tears and Dad doesn't say anything except to ask Lynn to call the elevator. We enter in silence and go down to the parking lot. We get in the car and Dad drives in the direction of the cemetery. The silence is so complete that I'm almost afraid to breathe. We're all lost in our own thoughts. I'm thinking about the cemetery. I've never been to a funeral before. I'm scared. My head is full of questions. What's it like to stand beside an open grave? Do I have to talk to people and if I do, what should I say? Will I see Grandpa's body? Will they put it in the ground while we're there? Just thinking about that makes me feel dizzy. The person I really need now is Grandpa, the only one who really knows how to make me feel better. I feel worse than I have ever felt. I feel I've lost all my hopes and all my dreams. I'm not even interested in Zoe. I'd do anything to bring Grandpa back. My face is covered with tears and I look down at my lap.

Suddenly I have the strangest feeling that Grandpa is with me, giving me strength. I don't understand what I'm feeling, but it's very strong. Dad drives into the parking lot of the cemetery and parks in the shade, near the sign. Mom gets out and motions to Lynn to join her. Where are they going? I stay in the car with Dad. We don't speak. Sometimes the best thing to do is to keep quiet. Grandpa always said that silence is the loudest sound. I never understood what he meant before, but now I feel as though I do. Mom and Lynn come back with a big bouquet of flowers and some candles.

If we were in a different place, you might think we are at a graduation party at a school – there are so many people. I hear lots of people crying. I can't tell if they're all crying for Grandpa or if other people have died as well and they're also being buried today. I don't dare ask anyone. I see some of our relatives and I see Mom hugging Uncle Eric and his wife, Aunt Rickie. I see groups of people a little way off and I realize that there are other funerals here, too. All the people standing near me are crying and trying to get close to Mom to hug her, but no one notices me. I move to stand on the side.

The minister starts to read from his prayer book and then I notice a wrapped-up shape on a stretcher. It looks like it could be a person. It's

Grandpa! I feel something strange is happening to me. Then I look up and I see Grandpa standing a little way off. He's looking right at me and calling my name. I start to shake all over and I look down again. What's happening to me?

Slowly, I raise my head and there's Grandpa smiling at me. "Andy my boy, I'll never leave you."

I feel like I'm going nuts. On the one hand, I'm shaking all over, but I can't move. Grandpa keeps talking to me. I'm frozen on the spot. All the people around me are crying. Dad's hugging Mom and Lynn's holding Aunt Rickie's hand. I don't understand what's happening to me. I'm positive that I'm losing it.

Now I see Grandpa floating above me, smiling his usual smile and speaking in his usual direct way. "Andy, listen, no one can see me except for you. Try to calm down. I promised you that I wouldn't leave you until you're Zoe's boyfriend."

"Grandpa, don't leave me," I beg.

He stretches out his hand to me. "I'm going to stay with you, Andy, and you have hugs and kisses from Grandma."

I feel dizzy and everything is spinning around me. The sounds of crying are getting louder.

"He fainted!" I hear a shout. "Someone call an ambulance!"

Now Grandpa's standing beside Dad and talking to me, "Andy, you have to rest. I'll stay right beside you."

I try to tell him that it's not possible, he died yesterday. How can he be talking to me? But my throat's closed up again and I can't make a sound. Dad splashes water on my face from somebody's bottle. I sit up and Dad helps me walk over to a bench. I want to tell him that I can see

Grandpa and he's talking to me, but nothing comes out. I can't say a word. Dad strokes my head and asks Lynn to come. He hands her the car keys and asks her to get me settled on the back seat so I can rest. I follow her and she opens the door and I get in. I open the window and lie down. Lynn goes back to the funeral.

I take a few deep breaths and then I hear a familiar voice. "Andy."

I twist around and there's Grandpa, looking just like he looked yesterday, but his body is sort of see through. He manages to calm me down like only he knows how and tells me to breathe deeply again and stay silent. "No one can know that you see me."

"It can't be," I mutter.

"Andy, there are some kids who can talk to ghosts, especially if they were very close to the person who died."

"Why did you leave me, Grandpa? Why?" I start to cry.

Grandpa gently reminds me to stay calm. "I told you that I was ready to go, but I also promised you that I wouldn't leave you. I'm going to help you with Zoe."

"I don't care about Zoe," I say. "You are the most important person in the world to me and the best friend I have."

"But I'm with you, my dear, only with you." Grandpa smiles.

"So why did you have to leave me?"

"Andy, who are you talking to?" Mom is standing by the open window. It seems she heard everything.

I don't answer her and Grandpa puts a finger to his lips.

"No one," I mumble.

"I heard you talking to someone."

"I was talking to myself," I tell her, and then I understand. I'm the only one who can see Grandpa. I want to touch him.

Mom searches my face. "Come, we have to say goodbye to people." She opens the door and I follow her back to the cemetery. Grandpa walks along beside me. He doesn't say anything, but I can feel him there.

We say goodbye to the relatives and I hear Mom telling Aunt Rickie that she's worried that the visit to the cemetery was traumatic for me, because she heard me talking to myself. Rickie doesn't seem too concerned, maybe because she's a psychologist and she spends a lot of time around people who do weird things.

Grandpa is watching me all the time. Whenever I look around, I see him. We get into the car and Grandpa gets in beside me, then we all drive home.

Chapter Thirteen

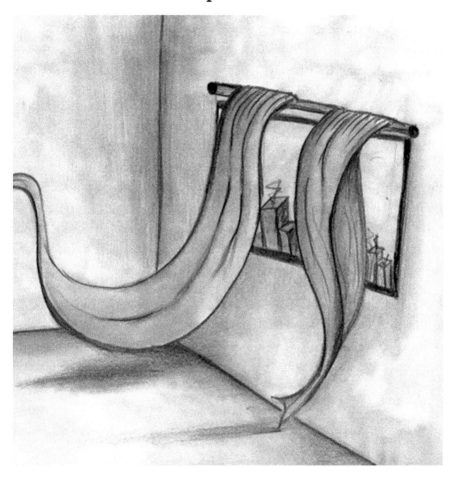

Ghost

When we get to our apartment, the front door is open. Dad peers round the door to see if anyone's there while I flatten myself against the wall. Mom says maybe she forgot to lock up. I go to my room and the ceiling light is flashing on and off as if someone's playing with the switch. It freaks me out. I walk in slowly and switch on the light and the flashing stops. Grandpa's ghost is sitting on my bed. He smiles and motions for me to come closer. I just stand there looking at him.

Mom calls from the kitchen and asks if I want something to eat, and I tell her no thanks. Then she says I should have a shower and put my clothes in the laundry. She says it's important to shower after you visit the cemetery. I don't understand why.

I go into the bathroom and shut the door behind me. Grandpa is standing next to the sink and I jump and cry out in surprise. Mom comes rushing to the door and asks if I'm okay, and Grandpa puts his finger to his lips again. I call through the door that I just saw a spider on the floor when I wasn't expecting it, but I'm fine now and I took care of it. It's the only thing I feel heroic about, especially since Mom and Lynn scream like two hysterical girls at a horror movie whenever they see one. I usually come to chase it away.

Grandpa grins. "Andy, I promised you a few things and I'll stay with you at least until they happen." I'm not sure what to say. I'm still not used to talking to a ghost. I would prefer to talk about other things, but Grandpa keeps mentioning Zoe. "You have to talk to her," he insists.

"I can't, she barely knows I exist."

"You have to make a move. Things don't happen by themselves; you have to make them happen."

"What am I supposed to do?"

"Talk to her tomorrow. Invite her to a movie."

That makes me smile a sad smile. "She'll never say yes. I don't stand a chance." I turn on the tap and the water starts flowing.

"You have to risk it."

"I don't know if I can. Actually, I'm sure that I can't."

Grandpa turns red and part of him becomes transparent. I'm scared.

"Listen to me," Grandpa insists. "You have to believe in yourself. It's the only way you'll get anywhere. If you don't believe in yourself…"

"No one else will believe in you," I finish the sentence and imitate his voice.

Grandpa takes shape again and smiles.

"Your belief in yourself will take you to great places. The only limits are the ones you place on yourself. If you want to succeed, you have to remember that the sky's the limit – you can keep going up and up, further and further. Everything is possible. It all depends on you."

A sharp knock at the door makes me jump. "Who do you think you're talking to?" Mom asks.

"No one," I answer.

"But I heard you. Come out. I want to talk to you," she says.

"Soon," I say and I get under the shower. For sure Mom will take me to therapy now.

After my shower, Grandpa's not in the bathroom anymore. I get dressed and go to the living room. Mom and Dad are in the kitchen. Mom's telling Dad how she heard me talking to myself twice today, once at the funeral and now in the bathroom.

"I'm so worried about him. We have to take him to see someone. I think he's experiencing a trauma." Yup, I'd better get used to idea of therapy again. Dad asks if she knows anyone really good to take me to, and Mom reminds him how much Janet helped me last time. She says

Aunt Ricky recommends her as well. "She's also a parapsychologist now, which could be helpful," she adds. Just the sound of that word is enough to terrify me. Mom keeps saying if someone talks to himself it may be a symptom of many problems, especially if it happens after a death.

I'll have to ask Tom to check out this parapsychologist, whatever that is. But I remember Janet, and I remember that I liked her. And who knows, maybe she can help me get Zoe to be my girlfriend. There has to be a good side to this.

We have an early supper but nobody says much. After we eat I go to my room and the light is flashing on and off again. Grandpa's ghost is sitting on my bed, waiting for me.

"Will you be sleeping over?" I ask hopefully.

Grandpa shakes his head.

"Will you come in the morning or at night?"

He doesn't reply.

"How can I call you?" I ask. He remains silent.

Suddenly Mom comes up behind me. "Who are you talking to?" she asks anxiously.

"No one, n-nobody," I stammer.

"Please go to sleep," she says. "You've had a hard day."

I lie on my bed. Grandpa's not there anymore. Mom sits down beside me.

"Andy, I'm worried about you. I think you need to talk to someone." Mom holds me tight and I feel so warm and safe. She kisses my forehead and switches off the light.

Through the open window I hear the wind moaning and howling, and it feels like someone's watching me. I pull the covers over my head and keep perfectly still. I close my eyes tightly and listen to the murmurs from the living room. I don't dare open my eyes. Worn out and confused, I finally drift off to sleep.

Chapter Fourteen

The Note

I wake up just when it's starting to get light. I look around me. I seem to be alone in my room. But then I see Grandpa. He's sitting on the edge of my bed. He pats the spot next to him and I scoot over, my heart beating hard in my chest. Grandpa talks, but I can't hear a word he's saying. I'm wondering who I can talk to about this. Not that anyone would believe me. Mom will definitely think I've gone nuts, and maybe she would be right. Grandpa talks on and on. I try to listen to him but I don't manage. Little by little I calm down.

When I look at the clock it's 6:52 a.m. Pretty soon Mom will come to wake me. Maybe I should pretend I'm sleeping. I look over at Grandpa and he's trying to tell me something. I tell him I'm going to talk to Zoe today. I can't wait to go back to school. Maybe we'll sit together on the bench and eat strawberries. I love strawberries! When I was little Grandma would always get them for me. Maybe that's why strawberry is my favorite ice cream flavor.

Grandpa smiles. "That's why I'm here," he whispers to me. "To give you the power to do it."

I feel brave. Yeah! I can do it. Yes I can! Andy will ask the beautiful Zoe to go to a movie with him. I'll do it today. Maybe I should write her a note?

Once again I don't notice Mom standing there. "Good morning," she sings out and I jump ten feet in the air. Mom walks over to me. "Who were you talking to?" she asks in her most concerned voice.

We lock eyes, but I can't say a word.

She puts her hand on my shoulder. "Andy, you have to talk to me about what you're going through. I want to help you."

"I was just talking to myself," I say gruffly. "I have to get ready for school now."

"Shall I make you some breakfast?"

"Yeah, I'm starving!" I want her to get out of my room, but when she's gone, I discover that Grandpa's gone as well. I'm sorry. There are so many things that I want to tell him. But I know he'll be back. I finish putting my books in my bag and I go to the kitchen. I can smell my omelet cooking and Mom is busy cutting vegetables for salad. When she cuts the onions my eyes fill with tears.

I eat fast, hoping Mom won't ask any more questions. Then Lynn comes into the kitchen. She says good morning to Mom.

"Hey. Are you just talking to yourself or do you have a new imaginary friend?" Lynn says in a baby voice.

"I was just trying to work out a tough math equation," I say . I hope that will remind her that I helped her out and that if she keeps up her teasing that help will disappear.

"Oh my god!" she says. "When will you start acting normal and think about girls?" She blows me a kiss and bursts out laughing. She always finds her own jokes very funny. Sometimes she's such an idiot.

Then things get even worse when Mom looks at me and says, "Andy, I've got to take you to talk to someone. A professional." I don't say a word.

"We are going to be staying at Uncle Eric's house during the day for awhile so people can come to visit and comfort us as we mourn Grandpa's death. But I'm worried about you. Maybe I should make an appointment for you today."

Lynn makes a face. "Definitely. You should take him." I think she's mad because I didn't laugh at her dumb joke.

Then I think of something – I go up to Lynn and whisper in her ear, "What's better, a heart or a smiley?"

She smiles at me and mouths, "A heart, obviously."

I stick my omelet between two pieces of bread, grab my bag and make for the door. Mom shouts that I haven't eaten anything, and I tell her I've made an omelet sandwich and I'll eat it on the way.

When I get to school I walk really slowly up the stairs. My legs are shaking and I must be talking to myself, because Stuart follows me into the class and I see everyone looking at me in a weird way. I have no idea why, but I hear Stuart laughing behind my back. Then he puts something on my head. I throw the hat across the room and sit in my usual place.

"Andy's talking to himself – or maybe he has a friend from another planet," Stuart shouts. Everyone laughs. As usual.

"Maybe his friend is ET," David says and all the boys near him burst out laughing.

I sneak a glance at Zoe – she's busy drawing in her notebook and she's not paying any attention to the boys. Does she also think I'm weird? Did Grandpa do something? All sorts of thoughts are spinning around in my head. I sit in my seat and take out all the things in my pencil case. I wonder how she would react if I really asked her, but as usual I'm too scared to even look at her.

"ET phone home!" Stuart calls out. And David agrees that ET is the best name for me.

I don't listen to them. I'm lost in my thoughts about Zoe. I have to write her a note, but what will happen if she shows it to everyone? Just the thought makes me break out in a sweat. Then Grandpa is suddenly standing in front of me and I jump in fright. The teacher just walked in. She calls my name and I don't react, everything goes blurry. I feel like I'm going to faint so I lay my head on my desk. I just want everyone to leave me alone. The teacher comes closer. I raise my head, and I'm sure she'll send me to the principal's office, but she just smiles down at me. She rests her hand lightly on my back and says, "I talked to your mother, try to be strong Andy." I don't understand exactly what she's talking about. Strong and me are two things that don't usually go together, but I nod my head.

Grandpa's still there. He's looking straight at me and he says, "Andy, you've got to write her a note."

I don't answer. I'm afraid everyone will see me and think I'm talking to myself. But Grandpa won't be ignored. He's as stubborn as ever. And I think to myself, "Today's the day." The teacher's writing on the board and all I can think about is what I should write to Zoe. Maybe something short like, "Want to go to a movie?" Or something long like, "There's a new movie you might like to see at the 3D cinema. What do you say?" Maybe I should draw a heart? Maybe I should say something to her? The fear paralyses me and I can't even turn my head in her direction. Grandpa's watching me all the time. I decide to write: "Do you want to come with me to see the new 3D movie?" I write in big block letters and I use a purple pen. Grandpa says all the pretty girls like the color purple so maybe that will help. It's almost time for the bell. I quickly pull out the page, tear it in half and fold it. The bell rings and Grandpa points at Zoe, but I can't move. He points at her with both his hands. It's a good thing only I can see him. I get up, my heart's beating hard and fast and I'm sure Zoe can hear it. I look straight at her and see that she's drawing in her notebook again. She's by herself. I move toward her, place the note on the edge of her desk and take off out the classroom door. Grandpa follows me all the way to the farthest bench in the schoolyard, where I collapse, completely winded. There's no one else around.

Grandpa's standing behind the bench. "Good for you! I'm proud of you!"

I turn around to face him and he's gone. I wanted to thank him but he disappeared too soon.

Zoe probably threw the note into the trash. I don't care, so long as she didn't show it to anyone. I'll die on the spot if anyone knows. If only she would say yes, or even just think about it. If only she doesn't say no. The bell brings me back to earth.

"Please don't let her say no. Please. Please," I mumble to myself all the way back to class. I get the shakes. I'm afraid to go into the classroom. When I'm almost at the door, the teachers' high heels click on the floor behind me.

Chapter Fifteen

Mrs. Hart

Mrs. Grant calls my name at least twice. She's the math teacher, tall and thin with straight black hair, dark skin, black eyes, white teeth and a strong, clear voice. I really like her classes, actually they're my favorite. Math is my subject.

Mrs. Grant comes over to me and smiles and her white teeth shine. She asks how I am and I nod at her to show that I'm okay. I'm still busy thinking about Zoe. Mrs. Grant asks me to go to see Mrs. Hart, the school counselor.

"Your mom's waiting for you in her office," she says.

I leave the class and start walking to Mrs. Hart's office. I actually feel relieved. Zoe's answer will have to wait until the end of the day. On my way, I stop at the bathroom. While I'm washing my hands I look up at the wall and see someone has written "Stuart and Zoe" inside a heart. That makes me mad and I erase it. As I approach the school counselor's office, the door is half-open. I see Mom sitting with Mrs. Hart.

I slow down to hear what Mom's saying. "He was very close to his grandfather. I'm worried about him."

Mrs. Hart listens intently. I bet she hears stories like mine all day long. "When someone close dies, it can cause all sorts of reactions. I suggest that you make an appointment with a psychologist." Since when does Mrs. Hart decide what treatment I need? I knock on the door and she sings out, "It's open!"

I push the door so it opens wide. Mom is wearing the same black dress she wore to the funeral. "It's nice to see you, Andy, please come in and sit down," says Mrs. Hart. "Tell me, how are you feeling?"

I shrug my shoulders.

"I'm sorry to hear about your grandpa. I understand that the two of you were very close."

I shrug again.

"I think you should go with your mom to see a psychologist; it can help at times like these." She keeps talking about how it's perfectly normal to feel disconnected from others and not to be able to function normally after someone close to you dies.

I can't follow anything she's saying because all I can think about is Zoe and the note I left on her desk and what her answer will be. Maybe she won't answer at all, but then I hope she doesn't tell everyone. Mrs.

Hart is still talking and she and Mom are looking at me anxiously. I'm counting the minutes until the bell rings and I can run outside to my bench in the schoolyard, where I can sit and watch Zoe and then I'll be able to tell whether she's told everyone or not and if they're all laughing at me.

Mrs. Hart says I can go back to my classroom and Mom gives me a kiss and a quick, tight hug. I walk really slowly on my way back to class. There's still time before the bell. I open the door and Mrs. Grant smiles and waves me to my seat. I keep my eyes to the front—I don't have the courage to look at Zoe—and I sit down.Sally gives me a big smile. I have no idea why, but it calms me down. No one knows anything I think.

Then I hear Stuart whispering to David, "ET came home."

David laughs. "So where's his spaceship?"

Without thinking twice I turn my head toward Zoe. Her eyes meet mine for a second and her expression is completely blank. It's clear she has nothing to say to me. My heart flutters and I feel dizzy. I must be insane. I want to ask Zoe out? Who do I think I am? I want to die. I only pray no one knows.

Sally nods at me and I have no idea what's going on, but I manage to fake a weak smile. Maybe she knows? Maybe she saw me writing the note? I curse Zoe inside. If she could hear what I'm thinking… When the bell rings I take off like a rocket, without looking behind me or to the sides. I wish I could disappear.

"Hey, wait up. Where are you running to?" I hear a familiar voice behind me.

Grandpa? I turn around and there he is. I keep running but he's right there behind me. That's all I need now, for everyone to see me talking to myself again.

"Well, did you talk to her?" Grandpa asks.

"I wrote her a note," I say.

"So what did she say?" Grandpa grins.

"She didn't say yes."

"Did she tell you why?"

"What does she need to tell me? She doesn't want me and that's it." I'm angry now.

Grandpa is perfectly calm. "That doesn't mean anything," he continues. "Exactly what did she say?"

"She didn't say a word. She looked straight through me and kept on going, as if I was air."

Grandpa never knew just how unpopular I am at school. I feel like I might explode.

"Maybe she's embarrassed?" Grandpa asks.

"Embarrassed? About what?" I don't get him. I mean, here's the Queen of the Class and I'm nothing. I don't count at all, I'm just some nerd.

"Just leave the movie ticket on her desk," Grandpa is still giving me advice.

I think about tomorrow; maybe I shouldn't give up yet. After all, she hasn't actually said no. My head starts whirling with numbers as I calculate how many hours there are until tomorrow and how much time it will take me to go buy tickets and which row she would want to sit in.

"What are you thinking about?" Grandpa asks.

And at that moment I hear a voice saying, "Andy, I'd love to go!"

I nearly jump out of my skin and Grandpa flattens himself against the wall. I turn around. Sally is standing there smiling at me. I still have no idea what she's doing there.

"I'd love to go to the movies with you," she says and she takes another step toward me. I can't make a sound. I try to speak but all that come out are these strange strangled noises. Sally holds out the note that I wrote to Zoe. I turn bright red. How did it get to her? "I'd be happy to go to the movie with you," she says again.

I silently curse myself with every curse I can think of and wish that I could wipe myself off the planet. Now that I realize what must have happened I break out in a cold sweat. Now I know why Sally kept smiling at me. I must have left the note I wrote for Zoe on my desk, next to Sally's, which means I left the blank half of the page on Zoe's desk. I can't look Sally in the eye. I zoom home, fly into my room, jump on my bed and scream.

Chapter Sixteen

Victor

Now what do I do about Sally? She's the nerdiest girl in the class. I finally get up the nerve to invite Zoe out on a date, and I accidentally leave a blank note on her desk and the note for Zoe on Sally's desk. Argh! I am so angry at myself. If Sally was my girlfriend we'd be the nerdiest couple that ever lived.

I hear someone guffawing loudly. I look around and there's Grandpa, sitting on the edge of my bed, his shoulders shaking with laughter.

"What's so funny?" I ask.

Grandpa tries to catch his breath. "You took off like a rabbit!"

"I made a huge mistake. I invited the girl in my class who's the biggest nerd in the world, instead of the prettiest girl, like I wanted to."

Grandpa stops laughing. "That's called Murphy's Law," he tells me. "It's when everything that can go wrong, does go wrong. Some people make every mistake that can possibly be made. But I'm still proud of you for trying. Now we have to decide what to do next to get things back on track."

"No chance," I say. "It's hopeless. Zoe will never want me. You should have seen how she looked at me. As far as she's concerned I don't even exist."

"Stop it," Grandpa insists. "You have to believe in yourself, or else…"

"No one will believe in you," I finish off his favorite sentence.

By the time I notice Mom in the doorway listening to our conversation, it's too late.

"Andy, who are you talking to?"

"To Victor," I reply.

Mom's jaw drops. "To Victor?"

"He's back," I tell her.

"Since when?"

"Ever since Grandpa died," I lie.

Mom comes to sit beside me on my bed and almost squashes Grandpa. I want to tell her to move over, but I can't speak. She strokes my head.

"We have to go to talk to Janet. She'll help you again, sweetheart. I'm so worried about you."

I nod.

"Is Victor here now?" she asks.

I shake my head no.

I think my imaginary friend Victor was with me from the day I was born. He would always come with me everywhere I went. For the longest time, he was my best and only friend, but because of him, Mom took me to see Janet. Janet's a psychologist and she tells everyone to call her by her first name. We talked a lot about Victor, and she told me it was important that I make other friends as well.

When Tom and I became friends, Victor started to slowly disappear, until he was showing up only once a week, then once every two weeks, and in the end, only on special occasions. He stopped coming when I was in fourth grade. At first I really missed him. I wrote him letters and drew him pictures of hearts with wings. The hearts had eyes shaped like hearts and a mouth shaped like a heart. I never had a better friend than Victor. I could tell him everything, even the curses I sometimes thought about but never said out loud. If he were to come back now, I would tell him about Zoe.

A sudden cool breeze twists the curtain, and my heartbeat speeds up like crazy. Mom holds me and I feel a bit better.

"I'll make an appointment with Janet. You aren't going to school tomorrow."

That cheers me up. Now I won't have to see Sally and maybe she'll forget all about the movie or change her mind. I have to write something crystal clear to Zoe. Or maybe I should just go up to her and ask her to come to a movie with me. My brain starts spinning love equations for me and Zoe, but none of them have a simple solution. What should I do?

Mom says I should come and eat something and then go straight to bed. It's 7:23 in the evening.

I eat some leftover meatloaf and mashed potatoes. Then I have a shower, get into my pajamas, and brush my teeth.

When I go back to my room, I can tell that Grandpa isn't there anymore. Mom sits with me until I fall asleep. She pulls up my covers and says, "When you lose someone you love, he never really leaves you; he stays with you in a special place, deep in your heart."

"I don't want Grandpa in my heart. I want him here," I say.

"I know," Mom says.

Shadows fall over my room and I know Grandpa's back.

Chapter Seventeen

Zoe

Zoe and I are flying at top speed, like Superman and Wonder Woman. I fly ahead and she's right behind me. My blue cape with a big A on it flaps in the wind, and Zoe's cape is red with a silver letter Z. We're both heroes and we save people every day. This time we're searching for survivors of a shipwreck. But how can we find them when the sea is full of mangled pieces of the boat that broke up on the rocks in the storm?

Dad's phone rings in the living room and I wake up. It's 9:34 in the evening and I've only been asleep for about an hour. Dad and Mom are sitting on the couch in front of the TV. When he finishes his call, Mom asks him if he wants something to drink and he says black coffee. That's what he likes best. I peek through the crack in the door. Mom puts the kettle on and while the water is boiling, she puts some cookies on a plate . Dad is already deep into the sports channel. He loves sports and he loves to talk, the two exact things that I'm worst at. I'm like Mom. Actually, I'm like Grandpa.

Mom sits beside Dad and asks him to turn off the TV. "I want to talk to you, it's important," she says.

"Can it wait?" Dad asks.

Mom shakes her head. "Victor's back."

Dad's silent. It's really not like him to stay so quiet.

"How do you know?" he asks in a shaky voice.

"Andy told me. I'm worried. I called Janet and we have an appointment for tomorrow. After she treated Andy a few years back, she studied parapsychology. That may be just what he needs now." "What's 'parapsychology'?" Dad asks. I'm glad to hear he doesn't know either. It still sounds like some ancient curse.

"I mentioned it to you before, weren't you listening?" Mom sighs. "It's when you try to understand what's beyond," Mom speaks really softly, but I can still hear everything.

Beyond what? What's she talking about? I run back to my room and jump into bed. A sharp wind whips around my room and when I look up at the ceiling, there's a huge jelly-like shape swirling around up there. It twists and turns and undulates like it's doing a crazy dance.

I want to scream, but of course – no voice. I huddle against the wall. That jelly thing comes closer until it touches me and I feel its stickiness. I close my eyes, and I am surprisingly calm. I stay that way for a while, and when I open my eyes again, I have a fuzzy feeling inside, and the giant jelly has faded away.

Then I hear Dad's voice from the living room telling Mom, "Tomorrow, after the meeting with Janet, we'll buy him a bicycle."

"Yes," Mom agrees, "we need to make him as happy as we can."

I close my eyes and a warm sensation floods my insides. I feel loved. I imagine riding my new bicycle to the beach with Zoe on the back, her hair flying in the wind and her arms around my waist. On the way, we pass Stuart and he whistles to us. David rides past on his bike and shouts, "Hey guys!" Zoe's laughter tickles my neck and, for that one dream moment, the feeling of being different from everyone disappears.

Chapter Eighteen

Janet

I haven't seen Janet for a long time and I still like the way she looks. She has long brown hair, big green eyes and creamy skin. Mom comes in with me and talks to her while Janet's cat Paris runs around the room. I'm watching Paris when I notice Grandpa standing there, smiling at me. Mom leaves, saying she'll be back in an hour. Janet sits opposite me in a big comfy chair and watches me with a kind and patient expression on her face, which is round like a smiley. She asks how I'm doing. Janet has a soft deep voice that makes me feel calm. I tell her that everything's okay because I don't know what Mom has told her.

"I heard your grandpa died," she says sympathetically. "You were so close. It must be terribly hard for you now."

I nod without speaking and suddenly all Paris' fur stands on end as if she's been electrified. They say cats are sensitive to ghosts – could it be that she sees Grandpa?

Janet glances from me to the cat. "What do you see?"

"Nothing," I say.

"Andy, you can trust me. Whatever we talk about stays within these four walls." Janet has such a soothing voice. I believe her and I feel like telling her everything, but still I hold back. Grandpa is actually sitting right next to her, on the arm of her chair, his shoulder almost touching hers.

"Do you see something now?" she asks.

I shake my head no. Her eyes staring into mine look huge and her voice is insistent.

"Tell me, Andy."

Grandpa motions to me that I can tell her, and that gives me some confidence.

"I see Grandpa."

"Is he in this room?" she asks.

"Yes, he's right beside you."

Janet sits up straight. "Can you talk to him?"

"Yes. He's with me a lot, and he helps me." I'm surprised by how much I'm telling her.

"There are people who, when someone really close to them dies, continue to see that person. Sometimes that person helps them out and even gets involved in their lives. What does your grandpa look like?"

"He looks the same as always, but sometimes, when he gets upset, bits of him disappear," I say, and then Grandpa starts talking. "Grandpa says to tell you that you're a good woman." That makes Janet smile. "But please, don't tell Mom."

"It's our secret, I promise," she replies. She puts her three middle fingers together and gives the scout salute. "You can count on me."

That makes me feel better. She believes me; I can tell her everything. Maybe I can also tell her about Zoe? Is there a chance that she'll help me? It feels so good to be able to talk to someone about this.

"There are people who can talk to spirits, and they are usually very special people," Janet speaks softly. What does she mean? Is she saying that I'm special? Grandpa looks pleased. He always says that I'm special.

"What do you and Grandpa talk about?" Janet asks.

"About everything," I say.

"Did he send you any kind of message?"

"Nothing special." I don't want to mention Zoe. At least not yet.

"Where do the two of you meet?"

I shrug. "Any place."

Janet jots something down in her notebook. "Can you contact him?" "No, he just shows up."

"Ask him if he has a special message."

"Right now?"

"Yes, Andy."

I feel silly. I look at Grandpa and ask him if he has an important message for us. He tells me his message is that he has to help me with Zoe and make sure I get invited to birthday parties. I repeat most of what he says, but I don't mention the part about Zoe. Janet says it's fine if Grandpa stays to help me with the things he promised. Finally, I feel like there's someone I can trust.

"You can call me whenever you feel like it and talk about anything you want," she says, handing me her new card with her name and number printed on it. She looks up at the big clock on her wall. The time is 11:57 in the morning; I have three more minutes.

I'm standing up and getting ready to leave when she suddenly asks, "Have you seen Victor recently?"

I freeze and a knot forms in my stomach. Why is she asking about Victor? I basically said goodbye to him in this very room.

There's a knock at the door. Janet calls out, "It's open."

Mom comes in. I move toward Janet and whisper in her ear.

Chapter Nineteen

David and Stuart

On the way home, Grandpa joins Mom and me in the car.

Grandpa and I sit in the back seat, and he starts talking to me about how important it is that kids who ride bicycles remember to wear a helmet. Mom is listening to the news on the radio and she doesn't seem to notice that I'm whispering.

"Hardly anyone wears a helmet," I say.

Grandpa gets angry. "One bang on the head can kill you. You mustn't ride without a helmet. A helmet can save your life. Simple as that."

I'm surprised by how adamant he is. Why is Grandpa talking about bicycle helmets all of a sudden? Does he know they want to buy me a new bike?

"I want to talk to you about Zoe," I whisper, changing the subject. "I'm in love with her."

Grandpa leans back on the seat. "You're making progress," he says.

"But she'll never want me."

Grandpa moves toward me and I feel him touch me, a weird feeling that makes me dizzy. "It's going to work out," he whispers.

"How do you know?" I ask.

But Grandpa doesn't answer. He just has this satisfied expression pasted on his face.

Mom stops the car at my school. My heart starts pounding against my ribs when I think about facing Sally. I have to say something to her. I get out of the car and wave goodbye to Mom. Grandpa comes with me, and since it's almost recess, we walk to the benches. We sit on my favorite bench, far away from everyone. I keep my back to the school, so they won't think I'm talking to myself again.

Grandpa says I have to tell Sally the truth.

"I can't do it," I say.

Grandpa won't give in. "Tell her the note was really for Zoe."

"I'm afraid I'll hurt her feelings."

"You'll hurt her more if you don't tell her."

I hang my head. "But I'm a coward!"

"No you aren't! And if you want Zoe, you have to tell her."

"Maybe you can tell her," I suggest.

"I can't. She can't see me."

"I don't think I can do it.

Grandpa and I are busy discussing this when someone gives me a rough push from behind. I tumble off the bench, hitting my side, and scratching my face on the prickly bush growing next to it. My ribs sear with pain. As usual, my glasses get knocked off and I can't find them because I can't see.

I hear David's familiar laughter. "ET, are you talking to your friends in outer space?"

My hands search the rough ground for my glasses.

Stuart shouts, "He has blood on his face." He reaches down and hands me my glasses.

I sit on the bench again and put on my glasses. Stuart and David come into focus in front of me.

"Well, ET, that's what you get for talking to yourself." Stuart smirks.

I touch my face and my hand comes away covered in blood.

David leans in and glares threateningly. "Watch out! You better not tell on me, or else I'll…"

"Enough, leave him alone," Stuart says.

I go wash up in the bathroom and David follows me. He puts his finger to his lips and then makes a slashing motion with his hand across his throat. When we walk out, Stuart is riding past on his bike.

"Don't ride without a helmet," I mumble.

Stuart looks surprised. "Don't say a word," he says.

"I promise, but wear a helmet."

"Okay. I promise, too," Stuart says and he takes his helmet out of his backpack.

Chapter Twenty

I'm Not a Snitch

To my surprise, the classroom's empty.

I pass a kid in the corridor who says the teacher's sick so they let everyone go home early. Good luck for a change – Zoe won't see me with my scratched-up face.

On the way home, I let Grandpa know I'm not going to tell on David and Stuart, but he says I have to, because David deserves to be punished.

"But I promised Stuart I wouldn't tell. I'll make up a story for Mom. I'll say I borrowed someone's bike and I fell off. But then she won't want to get me a bicycle. Oh well, the main thing is not to be a snitch."

"You can't let them get away with it," Grandpa says.

"Maybe Stuart will be my friend some day?"

"You're such a sucker!" Grandpa says.

The comment makes me mad. But with Grandpa I don't only shout inside. When I'm with him I can let it all out and say what I feel. I can yell and scream and I know he'll understand.

Grandpa yells back, but now that he's a ghost, when he shouts his voice sounds heavy. "You can't give in!" he insists.

We leave the elevator and I unlock the front door. No one's home. I wash my face and it doesn't look too bad. My arm hurts a bit, but I feel better. Grandpa walks around on the ceiling, humming to himself.

"Grandpa, I don't know what to do about Sally," I call up to the ceiling.

"Tell her you're in love with Zoe."

"Yeah, right. It's as simple as flying to the moon."

"Let me tell you a secret: A lot of things seem impossible until you do them."

"Okay! Tomorrow I'll tell Sally that the note was for Zoe. Tomorrow I'll tell her that I'm in love with Zoe."

I say that to myself a few times to get used to the idea. I go to the kitchen and get a bowl of strawberries. When I return to my room, Grandpa's sitting on the bed.

"So what did you decide to do?" he asks.

"To write a note to Sally."

Grandpa smiles. "Andy, you don't have much luck with notes."

"I just can't say it to her face."

"You haven't even tried."

"I don't have the guts."

While I'm talking to Grandpa, Lynn comes home. She's standing at the door to my room.

"Who are you talking to?" she asks.

I whip around to look at her. "T-t-to Victor," I stammer.

Lynn laughs. "Send him my regards and tell him to stop beating you up."

As she walks away, I get out paper and markers and make a big sign: Helmets Save Lives!

Mom comes in and asks me if I'm hungry.

"I ate some strawberries," I say, hoping she won't notice the scratches.

"Andy, look at me," she says, trying to get me to face her.

I try to keep my head down, but I can never hide anything from Mom. She always knows. I lift my head and look at her.

"What happened to your face?" she asks anxiously.

"I fell off someone's bike." I'm sure now I'll never get a bike of my own. But I don't want to be a snitch.

"Who let you ride?"

"Stuart," I lie.

"Where did you fall?"

"At school."

"I don't believe it Andy," she says.

I have to keep going so I show her the sign I just made. She looks at it suspiciously.

"Victor was really mad," I add, to sound more convincing. "He told me I have to be more careful and that I have to remember to wear a helmet."

"So promise me and Victor that you'll never ride without a helmet again," Mom says.

"I promise you both. I promise."

Chapter Twenty One

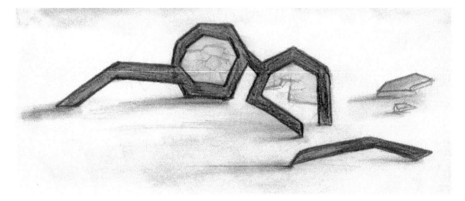

Helmets save Lives

The minute I walk into class I know something unusual is going on.

"Stuart's hurt," Sally tells me, wide-eyed.

"What happened?"

"I don't know, but I heard they took him to the hospital."

I look over to where Zoe sits to see how she's reacting to the news, and she looks just as worried as everyone else. I want to know more details. I look at Stuart's seat and I see Grandpa sitting there, pointing to his head, as if he knows that Stuart's been hurt. My stomach sinks. I hope Stuart wore a helmet, like he promised me. The bell rings and the literature teacher comes in. She writes in big capital letters on the board: **HELMETS SAVE LIVES!**

I don't understand why she wrote that, and then Zoe asks how Stuart is doing.

Mrs. Singh says, "He's lucky he was wearing his helmet. It saved his life."

Grandpa gives me the thumbs-up and a big grin. At that moment, Zoe's eyes meet mine. We look at each other for a few seconds. If only she knew that I saved Stuart. For a minute I feel like a real hero, and then I see Sally looking at me. I try to smile at her but I hardly manage. My expression freezes in a fake grin. I have to tell her. I shift my gaze away from her.

Grandpa sits on my desk and points to Sally. I can't react. I can't just start talking to him when other people are around. Mrs. Singh is still talking about safety, and I'm thinking about Stuart. Maybe he'll be my friend now and then I'll tell everyone that I told him to wear a helmet. I want him to come back to school already.

"When is Stuart coming back?" Zoe asks.

And the teacher says, "Maybe as soon as tomorrow."

Why is Zoe asking about him so much? Why her, of all the girls? Maybe she likes him. Maybe there's really no point in me even trying with her. Maybe I should just go with Sally. The bell rings and everyone leaves the class and I'm alone with Grandpa.

"When are you planning to talk to her?" he asks.

"At the end of the day."

"Maybe you *should* write her a note."

"I dunno."

"Get going, write it." Grandpa urges me.

I'm scared. What if someone else from the class reads my note? In the end I'm convinced. With Grandpa it will be easier.

"I need to think."

"Just write the truth. Instead of saying it, write it."

"Thanks for reminding me about the helmet," I say to Grandpa.

"I'm here for you."

It's the first time I feel strong. Maybe soon I'll get invited to birthday parties.

I tear a page out of my notebook and write: Dear Sally, I'm sorry, but the note I wrote was meant for Zoe. My apologies, Andy. I fold the note and leave it on Sally's desk.

Chapter Twenty Two

Almost Popular

Sally walks into the classroom grinning. The minute I see her, I grab the note and stuff it in my pocket.

Grandpa gets angry. He tries to push my arm, but the note is already deep in my pocket.

Sally looks at my face as though she's searching for something. I look at her, but I don't say a word. Grandpa is sitting on my desk. I can't concentrate and I'm just counting the minutes and seconds till the bell. Grandpa is talking non-stop, but I'm afraid to answer him.

Everybody starts laughing. I look over at Zoe and she's laughing, too.

The teacher walks over to me. "Andy, you aren't with us. Pay attention."

I don't answer her. Grandpa vanishes. The teacher warns me that if it happens again she'll call my parents. That's all I need. I try hard to concentrate, but I can't take in a word. If I give the note to Sally, she'll show it to all the kids and they'll laugh at me. Since when do nerds write love notes? But if I don't give it to her, she'll want to go to a movie with me and then I'll never be Zoe's boyfriend. I look at Zoe. She's drawing in her notebook. I wish I could see what she draws.

That's it. I've decided. I'll give the note to Sally at recess.

Sally is really focused on the lesson. It's a good thing she has no idea I have a volcano inside me. I count the seconds. There's less than a minute left until the bell. My heart is hammering so hard I'm afraid Zoe can hear it.

The bell rings and everyone hurries to recess. I ask Sally to wait a minute. When she turns around I hand her the note. After she reads it, her face crumples up and she blushes. In a hoarse voice she says, "You're just a weird boy."

"I'm sorry. I need to be alone now," I say and I walk away quickly. It's the first time I've ever felt like I'm not a nerd. I didn't like hurting her feelings, but I followed my heart.

Chapter Twenty Three

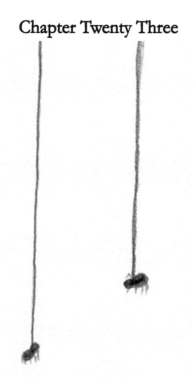

Sharing a Secret

Grandpa and I are walking home together.

"I feel bad that Sally's upset now, because of me," I tell him.

"It's better that she knows the truth," Grandpa replies firmly. "The truth never lies."

I "But sometimes it hurts."

Someone touches me from behind and I jump. It's Tom.

"Who are you talking to?" he asks me.

"Never mind," I say. "Sorry, Tom, but I kind of feel like being by myself right now."

"Hey, I also feel like being alone, let's be alone together." Tom playfully punches my arm. "Come on. Tell already, who were you talking to?"

"Promise you won't tell anyone?"

"I swear."

"I'm talking to Grandpa's ghost." Tom's eyes widen. "How cool! What, is he here? I want to shake his hand." Tom stretches out his hand and touches Grandpa's shoulder. I move it so it's lined up with Grandpa's hand.

"Grandpa says you're a smart kid," I tell Tom.

Tom grins and his cheeks turn red. Then Grandpa disappears. Tom's still standing there with his arm outstretched in the middle of the street. I see some kids from our grade coming toward us and I quickly push down his arm.

"Let's play on the PlayStation at my house, and you can tell me about ghosts," Tom suggests.

"I already told you," I say impatiently.

"You know, some people hold séances so they can talk to friends and relatives who have died. They use a special Ouija board and they call the spirits so they can talk to them. There are more than 1500 séances held every day in the US. Just so you know, there are other people like you who can talk to ghosts," Tom tells me. "Hey, my parrot died last year, can you see him?"

"I don't want to talk to any parrot," I say.

Zoe and Maya pass us on the street. From the way they're dressed, I guess they're going to dance class. All the popular girls go to dance class. I've never seen Zoe dance, but she looks so good in her black leotard. I don't want her to see me, but I don't have time to disappear around the corner to my street, so instead of walking like a normal person, I freeze in place like a statue.

She's busy talking to Maya and when they get closer she just says "Hi!" and keeps on walking. My whole body is burning up.

"Forget her. She's not for you," Tom says.

I remain frozen on the spot. How does he know? Is it so obvious? I start walking again and I pretend I didn't hear what he said. I don't feel like telling him about Zoe anymore. It's enough that I told him about Grandpa. But I definitely want to talk to Grandpa about this.

Chapter Twenty Four

The Third Eye

We go to my house. Tom asks if I have any Oreos and I take eight, four for each of us, from the cupboard in the kitchen. He sits on my bed and swallows his four cookies without hardly chewing, making happy smacking noises. He's practically sitting on Grandpa, but of course he doesn't know it.

Grandpa starts talking to me about Zoe.

"You're right," I say to him, "it's time I made some progress."

Tom doesn't know what I'm talking about. He looks confused.

"Grandpa asked how it's going with the math workbook," I lie.

"Hey, can your grandpa see the future?" Tom's getting excited.

"What do you mean?"

"Like, does he know who'll be the next world champion chess player, or what the winning numbers will be in the Lottery?"

Grandpa is busy playing with the PlayStation he got me for my birthday. It's pretty funny watching a ghost play on a PlayStation. I can't take my eyes off him.

Tom asks what I'm staring at.

I point at the PlayStation. "He's playing a game. You know, he's much better as a ghost. Before when we played together I would always win, but it looks like he's going to win now."

I ask Grandpa about the Lottery and whether he can see the future . He smiles. "I can't know what's going to happen in your world in the future, but I have connections where I am now."

I tell Tom what Grandpa said and his eyes shine. "Can you ask him if there's water on the moon?"

Grandpa laughs. "Your friend is clever. He should build a parabola."

"Build a parabola?"

"A parabola is a geometric shape," Tom explains." You build one by concentrating rays of light in such a way that you can burn up anything that tries to attack you." Then Tom starts talking again about holding a séance and using an Ouija board to talk to ghosts.

"So I could talk to Grandpa that way as well?" I ask.

"Yes, but it can be dangerous," Tom warns. "You might contact a bad spirit by mistake. I've read about spirits that harm people or take revenge on them for things that happened while they were alive. They say after people die, their spirit stays on earth for forty-two days." I can tell Grandpa is paying close attention.

"Grandpa only does good things," I say.

"There are good ghosts and bad ones," Tom says. "Did you know that dogs and cats can see ghosts?"

"For real?"

"When a cat starts going nuts for no reason, or when a dog starts chasing after nothing, you can be sure they're seeing a ghost. You're so lucky you can see ghosts, it's because your Third Eye is open."

"Third eye? If anything, I'm a four-eyes with my glasses, and anyway, I don't have any third eye."

Tom laughs. "Everyone has a Third Eye, but only special people know how to use it."

"So where is it?"

"In the middle of your forehead."

I touch my forehead, but I don't feel anything. Grandpa reaches out his hand and touches Tom, but Tom doesn't react.

"Your Third Eye is definitely closed," I say. "Grandpa just touched you, but you obviously didn't feel anything."

Tom starts feeling around in the air again, trying to shake Grandpa's hand. He looks really funny.

Lynn and her friend come home and they walk past my room and see Tom waving his arm around. They start laughing and Tom is really embarrassed.

"Now your sister will never stop laughing at me." He blushes.

"Get away from here," I scream, but Lynn ignores me and they keep on laughing. "Scram!"

Lynn walks away laughing.

"The nerds are really weird this time of year," her friend says.

"Yeah – too bad we didn't know they'd be putting on a show," Lynn says. "We could've sold tickets." They keep laughing as they close the door to her room.

"Hey, you never used to talk back to her like that," Tom says, impressed.

"I guess it's about time I started," I say. I watch Tom scarfing down my cookies. Chocolate and cream are smeared all over his face. "What do you want to be when you grow up?" I ask.

Tom wipes his mouth with his sleeve. "I want to win the Nobel Prize."

"What's that?"

"It's a prize you get for exceptional research or a new invention."

"Do you have an idea?"

"Sure." Tom grins. "I'm going to do research about ghosts."

We play chess. I'm black. I'd never beat Tom before when I was black. Grandpa shows me the moves and I beat Tom for the first time. I feel pretty proud of myself. Grandpa always hoped I'd be a serious chess player. You need to practice a lot and to be able to play against yourself, and the truth is I'm sick and tired of playing against myself. Maybe it's because of Zoe.

Chapter Twenty Five

Zoe Pulls a Muscle

Stuart is back in school. His scratches are almost healed, but his left arm is in a cast from fingers to elbow. The kids crowd around him holding colored markers. They all want to sign his cast. I look for Zoe, but I don't see her. It seems she didn't come to school today. Grandpa stands right in front of Stuart and examines his face carefully. He gives me the thumbs up to let me know that everything looks fine. I wait for Stuart to notice me and tell everyone how I saved him. It could be the moment I've waited for my whole life. The moment when I'm a hero.

Grandpa motions that I should move closer to Stuart. I stand right next to him.

He looks at me and smiles. "Hi."

I feel like I'm choking. That's it? He doesn't even ask me to sign his cast. I'm burning up inside, like a volcano full of boiling lava. I curse him silently with every curse I can think of. Lucky for him he can't hear them.

The bell rings and I go back to my seat. Sally won't even look in my direction and Zoe still hasn't shown up, so Grandpa sits at her desk. I start to worry, maybe something happened to her?

The teacher invites Stuart to come to the front of the class to tell everyone what happened to him. His cast is already covered with signatures and pictures. Even Sally signed it. Only Zoe and I haven't. Stuart starts to talk and I get lost in thoughts about Zoe. If only I knew why she didn't come to school. I try to get Grandpa's attention, but he seems to be listening to Stuart. Zoe's one of the best-liked kids in the class, so there's no chance they won't tell us why she didn't come. I count the minutes until the bell. Stuart finishes his story and everyone claps their hands. It's not enough that he's the most popular kid in the class, now he's a hero. Teacher even calls him "A shining example of the importance of road safety."

As I get up and move toward the door, Stuart comes up to me. I look left and right, but there's no one else nearby. He's really coming to talk to me.

He smiles. "Thanks," he says. "Hey, want to draw something on my cast?"

Grandpa points to an empty space. "We have something in common," I say. "We're both lefties. We're the only lefties in our class. They say that's an advantage in sports."

"Yeah, but now I'm benched. I can't write, ride my bike, or play sports, I'm finished," Stuart says sadly.

I don't know what to draw on his cast to cheer him up. Maybe I should draw Zoe? Or a bicycle? Or a dog that can see Grandpa? In the end, I draw a funny dog with a big head and tiny teeth and I write: "Get Well Soon! Andy."

I am so happy. I wrote on Stuart's cast like everyone else.

And then I overhear Maya talking to the teacher and mentioning Zoe's name. My ears swivel like two satellite dishes.

"Zoe pulled a muscle in dance class. She can't even stand on her leg," Maya's saying.

I freeze on the spot and Grandpa does, too. I've got to ask Tom how long it takes to recover from a pulled muscle. I look over at Grandpa and he nods to show me everything's under control. He'll soon find a way to get Zoe back on her feet.

Chapter Twenty Six

$51,656.60

When I get home, Mom opens the door for me. That's unusual.

"What are you doing home so early?" I ask, surprised.

"I want to spend time with you. I know how hard things are for you right now."

Grandpa sits on the table, listening intently.

"I want you to start seeing Janet regularly. She can get you through this."

"Did you know that you can talk to Grandpa?" The words come out before I can stop them.

Mom's eyebrows rise. She probably thinks I've gone nuts.

"You can hold a séance and talk to his spirit," I explain.

"That's nonsense. People can't really speak to spirits. Who told you that?"

Grandpa winks at me.

"You really need to spend some time with Janet." Mom sighs. "She'll help you."

I don't say anything. I look over at Grandpa, and he starts talking to me.

"Mom, Grandpa asks if you can please turn down the air conditioner. He says he's freezing."

The lines crease on Mom's forehead and she looks really frightened. "Andy, you have to stop this. You have to accept that Grandpa's gone. He's dead."

"But I can see him."

"I don't believe you. I know you wish you could see him. I also do. But you have to stop this."

Grandpa and I go to my room. I slam my door behind us.

"She'll never believe me." I sigh.

"I have an idea," Grandpa says. "I'll tell you something that only your mom knows. Tell her that I told you that she just withdrew $51,656.60 from her bank account and that her secret code is 1948."

Mom's sitting at the kitchen table with a mug of coffee and a piece of chocolate cake. She glances up when I enter the room. "Shall we make another appointment with Janet, sweetheart?"

"Grandpa says you withdrew $51,656.60 from your bank account today, and that your secret code is 1948."

Mom starts to shake and she drops her mug. It falls to the floor with a crash, splashing coffee, and scattering broken bits everywhere.

Lynn comes in and shouts at me, "Look what you did!"

"I didn't do anything. Mind your own business for a change and get away from me!" I say.

She puts her hands on her hips and glares. "How dare you talk to me like that?"

"I'll talk to you any way I like," I say with my new confidence.

Suddenly Mom screams, "Lynn, go to your room right now!" We're both stunned. It's the first time Mom has ever been on my side.

Thanks Grandpa. Maybe the good guys really do win in the end.

Chapter Twenty Seven

Mom and Dad Know

I write note after note to Zoe and throw each one in the trash. None of them is good enough.

Grandpa's losing patience with me. "Just draw a heart with an arrow," he suggests.

"She'll either throw it away or show it to everyone. I have to invite her to a movie."

"So how hard is that? Why do you keep crumpling them up?"

"I need to write something so powerful that she'll agree to go to a movie with the class nerd."

"Maybe if you promise her she can meet a ghost," says Grandpa slowly, "then she'll agree."

"You are brilliant Grandpa. That's a very cool idea. But she'll never believe me."

"Just try."

"She'll think I'm out of my mind and she'll never come near me. I need to think about it."

I hear the front door open. Dad's home. Mom is still sitting in the kitchen, pale and frightened and confused. Dad kisses her on the forehead, takes a bottle of beer out of the fridge, and asks if something happened. She doesn't answer.

"How are the kids?" he asks.

She doesn't answer him. Then she calls me. I go to the kitchen. Grandpa follows me.

"Tell your father," she says.

"Tell him what?"

"What you told me."

I just stand there.

"Andy sees Grandpa," Mom says, her voice trembling.

Dad sips his beer. "Andy, you've got to stop this; enough with the imaginary friends and the ghosts. You need to get some help."

Grandpa whispers to me. I look at Dad and I say, "Grandpa asks why you haven't taken the car for its yearly tune-up, since you're eleven days late."

Dad's eyes open wide and the beer bottle slips out of his hand and crashes on the floor. He mumbles, "It can't be, it can't be…"

Chapter Twenty Eight

The Right Words

At breakfast Grandpa sits beside me at the table, checks out what I'm eating, and talks non-stop. I don't pay any attention to him. I shove my omelet between two slices of bread and grab my backpack. Mom shouts after me that I didn't eat breakfast.

"I'm taking it with me. I'll eat on the way," I call back. Grandpa walks beside me, explaining how breakfast is the most important meal of the day.

"No one eats breakfast," I say.

"Bad habits are at the root of every man's troubles," he lectures me. I don't respond. My head is full of thoughts about Zoe. Will she or won't she come to school today?

"I've got to ask her today," I interrupt him.

"You have to do something to make it happen," Grandpa says once again.

I take the note out of my pocket and show it to Grandpa, even though he already knows what it says: I have two tickets to the latest Harry Potter movie. Want to come with me? Andy."

Grandpa smiles. "I'm sure she'll say yes."

At least I'll finally know what she thinks of me.

My heart is beating a mile a minute as I walk through the school doors and I'm tingling all over, like when my leg falls asleep. I walk into my class and search for Zoe, but her seat is still empty. All the boys are standing around Stuart, the wounded hero. What, do they think he's a brave warrior come back from the wars? The guy just fell off his bike. I don't even say hi, but just go and sit in my place. Grandpa sits in Zoe's empty chair. He knows I always look over that way.

Mrs. Grant, the math teacher, comes in. It's a good thing we have math now because I wouldn't be able to concentrate on any other subject. She writes some equations on the board and I solve them before anyone else does. I notice that Grandpa's crawling around on the floor under Zoe's desk. What's he doing there? Maybe he'll find something that will give me a clue about what she likes.

The next half of the lesson is new material. It's really easy for me, because I've already covered it in the workbook from Grandpa. I know all the answers. Too bad Zoe isn't here today or maybe she would be impressed by my math smarts. For the whole recess Stuart talks about his bike accident and how close he came to getting killed. Instead of playing sports, he tells everyone how it's really cool to wear a helmet. He ignores me completely. I curse him silently and wish that everyone would stop listening to him. I wish they would find out the truth. Grandpa gets my attention with a new idea. He says I should phone Zoe to ask how she's feeling.

"But I've never called a girl before. Forget it," I tell him. "I'll wait till she comes back to school."

All the way home, Grandpa tries to convince me to phone her. "It's the easiest thing in the world. Much easier than writing a good note."

"No way," I say. "I can't do it. If she just says hello, I'll choke."

Grandpa gives it a rest and we go into the apartment. Lynn is sitting in the kitchen with one of her glamour girl friends. I say hi and go to my room, with Grandpa following close behind. I drop my backpack and fall onto my bed in despair. I wish Zoe would come back to school. I should phone Tom and get some information about pulled muscles.

The home phone rings. Lynn picks it up and shouts, "Andy, it's for you!"

For me? It can't be. Nobody ever phones me. I go to the living room and my stomach feels funny.

I say hello and a woman's voice asks, "Andy, is that you?"

"Yes," I say softly.

"Hi Andy, I'm Thelma, Zoe's mom." I can't breathe, I can't say a word. "Zoe hasn't been at school for a few days and Mrs. Grant said you would be her choice to help Zoe make up the material she's missed. Would you mind helping her to catch up with her math homework?"

Grandpa starts to sparkle. He lights up like fireworks on the Fourth of July. I want to shout with joy, but I'm tongue-tied. Grandpa motions to me that I should speak. Then he dances around me, walks up the wall, and along the ceiling, doing cartwheels in the air.

Zoe's mom repeats her question.

I finally manage to say, "Yes, I'll come."

She tells me the address and how to get there and asks if I can come at five o'clock. It's the best phone call I've ever had. I look at Grandpa. "Is this your work?" I ask.

Grandpa just smiles but his smile convinces me that it was he who found the perfect words to say.

Chapter Twenty Nine

The Lie

Mom comes home from work early again.

She knocks on my door. "Hi sweetie, I made an appointment for you with Janet for five o'clock today. So be ready to leave at half-past four."

I almost pass out. Today is the day that I'm supposed to go Zoe's house at five. There is zero chance that I'll go with Mom, but I keep quiet. What should I tell her? That at precisely five o'clock I'm going to meet the girl I love? Since when do I love a girl? I have to get Mom to move our appointment. The time is 3:04 in the afternoon. I have to come up with an excuse. I look at Grandpa but he doesn't say a word.

"You have to find me an excuse," I beg.

Grandpa suggests that I tell Mom that I have a meeting with a teacher at school.

"Not good enough," I say. She could send a note asking them to let me out of it."

Grandpa thinks for a minute and then a smile breaks out all over his face. "I have a great idea! Tell her that you've been invited to a birthday party."

I start to tremble and I feel that volcano inside. No one has ever invited me to their birthday party and Mom knows that. She probably won't believe me. Today of all days!

But I have no choice. I have to tell her something before it's too late. I go to her room where she's sitting on the edge of her bed with a chocolate bar in her hand. Grandpa follows me and gives me the thumbs up. I start to sweat. What will happen if she doesn't agree to cancel? I have to go to Zoe's. There is no way I'm not going.

"Mom, I have to tell you something," I say.

"What is it sweetheart?" she asks. She seems to be in a good mood. She's eating chocolate and that always puts her in a good mood. When she doesn't have any chocolate for a few days she gets super irritable and you can hardly say a word without her biting your head off.

"I can't go to see Janet today."

"But I've made an appointment, Andy. Listen, I really believe that she can help you again. It worked last time. You have to stop talking to Grandpa. Dad and I are very worried about you."

"Mom, I just can't go today."

"Andy," Mom says in her most stern voice, "we already have an appointment."

"I got invited to a birthday party." Mom is shocked into silence.

"It's Zoe's birthday party today," I plead, "at exactly the same time."

"Okay, sweetie, I'll try to change it to tomorrow."

"Thanks Mom," I say. I fly to my room and I want to scream aloud with joy, but I have one of my silent shouts instead, so Mom won't hear.

I'm the world's happiest nerd.

Chapter Thirty

The Fear

It's 4:04 in the afternoon.

I have to be at Zoe's in 56 minutes.

What I should say when she opens the door? Everything I can think of sounds totally lame. I ask Grandpa for a brilliant idea.

"Hi, how are you Zoe? I was really worried about you," he suggests. "Or maybe: I'm so happy to see you."

The truth is I'm not too impressed. They sound like things an old person would say. I have to say something much cooler, but what if I freeze? What if I don't manage to say a word? I'll probably trip over my tongue or stutter. Maybe I should write a note? No, that would be super nerdy. I'm burning up.

Grandpa tries to calm me down. "I'll be with you, take it easy. Believe in yourself. I'm sure you'll do fine."

"I can't go," I wail. "I'll call her mother and tell her I'm not coming."

Grandpa runs back and forth on the ceiling, then down the wall and stops in front of me.

"There is no chance that you're giving up."

"I've already given up!" I shout. "I can't move." the thought of going to Zoe's has me paralyzed. "And if she sees me like this, I'm finished. She'll never look in my direction after this."

I can tell Grandpa is angry, because his bottom half becomes transparent and his top half turns red. "The time is 4:12. In 18 minutes we are moving out," he says sternly" Get ready! Don't let yourself down!"

"The minute she opens the door I'm going to faint," I state. "Since when does a nerd knock on the door of the Queen of the Class?"

"Since today!" says Grandpa. "So get a move on!"

I put my pencil case in my backpack, along with the homework and the exercises from the past three days. At least I can show her how good I am at math I tell myself, but it doesn't make me feel any better.

Grandpa starts humming some love song and it really gets on my nerves.

"Stop it!" I shout. "I need quiet!"

"Fear is man's worst enemy."

"So what can I do about it?"

"Do the thing that scares you the most."

Chapter Thirty One

Bad Spirit

The time is 4:32. Grandpa keeps telling me to hurry up, but I just can't move.

Mom asks, "What gift do you want to bring to Zoe?"

I don't answer. I don't want my lies to start piling up.

Grandpa whispers in my ear, "I bought her a book."

I repeat what he said and Mom leaves me alone. Grandpa and I go out and I call the elevator. But once we're inside I can't press the button. Grandpa speaks right into my ear, "Come on Andy, or we'll be late."

I press the button marked 0 because that's the number I feel closest to right now. Zoe lives about fifteen minutes away. Of course, I've never been to her house, but Mom has a friend on the same street. My body drags like I'm a lead weight. I feel like I weigh about 400 pounds. I can hardly move. Grandpa chats to me nonstop, but I don't hear a word, as if we're separated by a glass wall. Now it's 4:39. We've been walking for five minutes. I feel as though I've just run around my school ten times.

"I can't go on! I'm going home!" I tell Grandpa.

"Never," he replies. "You have to keep going."

"I don't have the courage. I'm afraid. I'm definitely going to faint." My heart's beating so loud I expect people to gather around their windows to see what all the racket's about. Two kids walk past and start laughing, saying I'm talking to myself. Grandpa keeps encouraging me and I make it as far as the corner of Zoe's street. I take slow, heavy steps. The time is 4:47. In five more buildings we'll be there.

Zoe lives at number 18 on the sixth floor, in apartment 12. We reach the building and the front door is open. Maybe it's a sign? Maybe someone left it open for me? I walk into the lobby and press the button for the elevator.

"Believe in yourself. I'm with you." Grandpa smiles at me.

The elevator rides up to Zoe's floor. Stars float in front of my eyes, and all the buttons on the panel in the elevator seem to be coming toward me and changing color. Grandpa reminds me to get out when we reach the sixth floor. I stand in front of Zoe's door, staring at a sign that says "The Kerry Family".

Grandpa tells me to ring the bell, but my arms seem to be glued to my sides. I finally ring the bell. I hear footsteps coming toward the door.

The door opens slowly. Zoe's looking at me. "Hi."

I've turned to stone. The only thing moving is my heart trying to bust through my ribcage.

"Hi, Andy," she repeats. "Have you come to bring me the homework?"

I'm still mute and Grandpa runs screaming to the stairwell. I don't understand why he ran away. I can't believe he's given up on me.

Then I look up and I see him floating above Zoe's head. He's huge and black and he's glaring at me with enormous black eyes that seem to be trying to bore into me. I take a few steps back and he opens his huge mouth, filled with pointy black teeth and begins to speak. His voice is like a rusty door in the wind and he's holding a big box of matches as he says, "I'm going to burn down this house. They killed my son." I quake in fear.

Zoe calls my name again, but it sounds to me as if her voice is coming from far away. "Andy, why aren't you answering me?"

I turn and run. I fly down the stairs like a fighter plane with an enemy on its tail. I run all the way home without looking back. I'm sure he's right behind me.

Chapter Thirty Two

Saving Zoe

I burst into the house like a storm.

Mom and Dad are sitting in the living room with some friends from Dad's office.

"What happened?" Mom asks.

"Nothing!"

"Andy, what's going on?" Dad asks. Everyone's staring at me.

"I saw a giant scary man who said he wants to burn down Zoe's house," I tell them.

"What kind of man?" asks one of the guests.

"A big guy who burns down houses."

Mom says she doesn't understand what I mean and Dad's nostrils flare like an angry bull. "Andy, go to your room and don't come out again until you're ready to quit talking about all these ghosts and demons."

I go to my room and slam my door. I'm sure that little scene hasn't improved my status with Dad, especially now that I probably embarrassed him in front of his friends. Mom opens my door and comes in.

"Too bad Dad can't see what I see," I say.

"Your father's worried about you," Mom says as she strokes my head. "Don't worry, sweetie, tomorrow at five we'll go see Janet. I'm sure she'll be able to help."

"Mom, I really need to be alone." I sigh. She kisses my forehead and goes back to the guests. I sit on my bed trying to work out what just happened at Zoe's.

Grandpa appears, looking really freaked out.

"Why did you take off like that?" I ask.

"It's very dangerous."

"What's dangerous, Grandpa?"

"That bad spirit you saw. He stayed here to exact revenge." He shudders.

"Who does he want revenge on?"

"On whoever killed his son in a bicycle accident. His son was riding without a helmet," Grandpa explains.

"How do you know?"

"He came after me and he was shouting that he's going to get his revenge. But like I always tell you, the good guys win in the end, so after a tough battle I managed to get away."

"Now Zoe will think that I'm a nerd who's also insane and she'll never even look at me again, forget about talking to me."

"Stop talking nonsense," Grandpa says, now that he's recovered. "Everyone deserves a second chance."

"So what? Am I supposed to tell her that I ran away because I met an evil ghost looking for revenge at her house? She'll never look my way again."

"Andy, you have to save her."

"Me? Didn't you see how I ran away?"

"You've got to find a way to stop that evil spirit, or he'll harm Zoe and her whole family."

"Grandpa, I need your help. You have to give me an idea."

"I don't have a clue about how to fight evil spirits."

It's the first time I've ever heard Grandpa say that he doesn't have a clue about something. I'd better ask Tom. He'll definitely know how to fight evil spirits. I am going to save Zoe.

Chapter Thirty Three

Battle of the Spirits

I phone Tom. He's watching the science channel.

"Tom, I need you! It's urgent!" I shout.

"Just a second," he says, and he leaves me waiting on the line.

Grandpa's lying on my bed. He looks really worn out. I wonder if ghosts get tired.

Tom picks up the phone again. "What's happened?"

"You'll never believe it," I say, "You've got to help me."

"With what?"

129

"I need to know how to get rid of an evil spirit."

"An evil spirit?"

I tell Tom about everything that happened when I went to give Zoe the math homework.

"So what did you do?" Tom asks.

"I took off like a rocket and didn't look back until I was safe in my room. I was sure that black giant was right behind me."

"What did Grandpa do?"

"He took off before I did. You've got to help me save Zoe. He was really terrifying." I shiver. "Even Grandpa was afraid."

"I'll think of something and then I'll call you back," Tom reassures me.

Grandpa's still lying on my bed staring at the ceiling. His face looks frozen.

"Are you okay?" I ask him.

"I lost a lot of power in my fight with the big guy. We had a spirit battle and now I have to rest," Grandpa explains.

I don't know what to do. I'm worried about Grandpa and Zoe. I pray that Tom will know what to do. It's my only chance to save Zoe. If something happens to her, it's my fault. I lie down on the bed next to Grandpa and try to think about good things. The telephone rings and I grab it.

"I found something," Tom yells.

"What? Give!" I shout back.

"I'll tell you tomorrow, at recess."

"No way! I need to know now!"

"I found a spell that banishes evil spirits," says Tom, and he hangs up.

Chapter Thirty Four

The Secret Whisper Spell

Tom and I battle the black giant with spears and swords. He spits fire at us, and I dive to avoid the orange flames. Tom aims with his spear and launches it through the black hand. The giant bellows and laughs an evil laugh. He winds his spooky fingers around Tom's neck and starts to choke him. I run at him with my sword to save Tom.

"Help me!" Tom cries, his voice fading. "He's spitting fire bombs! They're huge!"

My alarm clock rings and I wake up in a cold sweat. I close my eyes again. I hear Mom and Dad talking in the kitchen. I open my eyes and see Grandpa pacing along the wall. I pull myself out of bed. The dream disturbs me. I hope Tom's spell works, or it's all over. I get washed and dressed and eat some strawberries. Mom reminds me that we're going to see Janet at five today. On the way to school I think about the black ghost. Grandpa is quiet. That scares me more than anything, because he never stops talking. Maybe I should talk to the school counselor after all? But she'll never believe me. If Tom's spell doesn't work, I'll tell Janet everything. Maybe she'll be able to help.

Then Grandpa says, "Your friend is a smart guy. I hope he finds a solution or it will be a disaster." I freeze. If Grandpa is this worried, I may as well give up now.

Then Grandpa starts talking again and he sounds more sure of himself. "We'll figure it out. I can feel it. Your friend will find the answer, my intuition tells me so."

There's always some fancy word to give you hope, I think to myself as I walk into class. It's almost nine o'clock and most of the kids are there. I look for Zoe and I see she's back at school, talking to Stuart. I get so angry when I see the way she's looking at him. If she only knew that I'm the one who saved him, she would look at me that way, too. I feel so jealous I wish he would break a leg. I wish he'd never be able to ride a bicycle again and never come to school. I just pray that Zoe won't look at me and laugh because that would destroy me. She probably thinks I'm Super Nerd, after I ran away like that. I've really blown it now. She's deleted me for sure.

Grandpa sits on the teacher's desk. I check out Stuart from the corner of my eye. Zoe's still talking to him. What are they talking about for such a long time? The bell rings and everyone sits down. I look over at Zoe. Someone else probably brought her the homework while I took off like a scared rabbit. She'll never know what I saw. I'm finished. I count the minutes till recess. Grandpa wanders round and round the board. I count the number of times he goes around, divide by the number of words written on the board, and get the number nine. The minute class is over I bolt for the door and run all the way to my favorite bench. Tom's already sitting there waiting for me, and Grandpa's right beside him.

133

"Is Grandpa with you?"

"He's sitting right beside you. Talk."

"Hi Grandpa," says Tom and he sticks his hand out in the air. "I found the way to banish evil spirits."

"You mean to get rid of them?" I ask.

"Yup."

"How?" But before Tom has a chance to tell me, Zoe and Sally walk past, laughing. What are those two doing together? They're probably laughing about me and my note. I quickly look away. Then I lower my eyes and wait until I'm sure they're gone. I grab Tom by the shoulders. "Tell me!"

"There's a spell you have to whisper thirteen times inside the house, and then the spirit will vanish."

Grandpa and I are wide-eyed. "How does it go?"

"I can't tell you now. I can only say it when we're on the way to Zoe's house."

"You've got to tell me," I insist.

"If I tell you before that it won't work."

"So when do we go?"

"Tomorrow at 7:13 in the morning we'll go to her house."

"No chance," I say.

"This is your chance to be a hero," Grandpa says.

Chapter Thirty Five

Super Hero

On the way to see Janet, I try to decide if I should tell her about Zoe or keep the whole thing a secret.

Grandpa says I have to tell her. He says I have nothing to lose – even if she doesn't help me, it won't hurt to tell her. I can't even whisper an answer to him, because Mom won't stop talking.

"Andy, tell her everything so she'll really be able to help you," Mom advises. Maybe Mom can see Grandpa now, too?

"Okay," I say, "I get it."

"You know that I love you so much?" Mom says. I feel warm and happy all over, but if Zoe said the same thing to me I would probably get so worked up that I'd cry. It doesn't matter, because it's never going to happen. I was born a nerd and I'll die a nerd. I'd do anything to fix things. I wonder if everyone really is entitled to a second chance, like Grandpa says. Mom stops the car outside Janet's office.

"She's waiting for you, Andy." Mom gives me a kiss on the forehead.

Grandpa and I get out of the car. "Tell her everything," Grandpa says again.

"I don't know…" I say.

"She can help you."

"How do you know?"

"Intuition." Grandpa laughs.

Janet opens the door with a welcoming smile. Her white teeth dazzle my eyes. "Hey Andy, how are you doing?"

"Okay," I say as I walk into her office.

Paris the cat yowls a long meeeowwww and circles my legs. Maybe she can see Grandpa, who is now walking all over the ceiling. Paris starts jumping up in the air. I sit down and Janet asks if I want something to drink. All I want is to save Zoe! Should I tell Janet? I don't know what to do. Grandpa is busy driving the cat crazy.

Janet looks at me and asks, "Is Grandpa here?"

"Yes." I nod. "He's here, walking all over the ceiling."

Janet shoos the cat out of the room. Grandpa comes down from the ceiling and sits next to me.

"Go on, tell her," he urges me.

"I have something to tell you, but you have to promise to believe me," I say to Janet.

"I'll believe you, Andy. You can say anything to me." Her soft voice makes me feel calm and safe. Even Grandpa looks more relaxed.

"There's a girl in my class named Zoe. She pulled a muscle in her dance class so she missed a few days of school. Her mom asked me to bring her the math homework." I tell Janet almost everything about Zoe. Then I take a deep breath. Should I tell her that I love Zoe? Is it important for her to know? I look over at Grandpa and he motions that I should tell her.

"Her mother asked me to come to their house yesterday at five o'clock. I went there and I rang the bell…"

"So that's why you changed your appointment…" I nod yes.

"What happened after you rang the bell?" Janet is watching me closely.

I'm starting to sweat as the fear returns and I remember what I saw. "When Zoe opened the door, I saw an enormous black spirit floating above her head. He talked to me!"

"What did he say?"

"That he was going to get revenge on whoever had killed his son." I'm shaking now. "And that he was going to burn down Zoe's apartment."

Janet's eyes narrow and she leans forward. "And what did you do?"

"I ran out of there like crazy," I said. And then I stop talking. We look at each other.

"Zoe's family must be warned," Janet pronounces.

"They won't believe it in a million years," I say.

"So maybe I should talk to them?"

Grandpa joins the conversation and says, "Yes, Andy, tell her to talk to them."

"No way, Jose," I say. "I am going to save Zoe."

"So what do you intend to do?" Janet asks me.

"My friend Tom found a spell that gets rid of evil spirits."

"How do you know it will work?"

"Look, if I don't save her, I'm finished," I tell Janet, and suddenly I feel sure that I can do it. I'm a superhero. "I'm sure I'll succeed."

"It's dangerous," Janet says. "Did the spirit tell you when he's going to do the evil deed?"

Grandpa pipes up again, "Tomorrow morning at 7:32. She has to do something."

I feel totally stressed. "How do you know?"

Grandpa runs up and down the walls of the room and then comes back to me. "There isn't much time."

"But how do you know?" I ask again.

"I know," he says. Grandpa never says a thing if he's not one hundred percent sure about it.

"Tomorrow at 7:32 in the morning," I tell Janet.

"There's no time. I have to warn them," she says, her face white as a sheet.

"Please, don't talk to them," I beg. "Do something else."

"But why?" Janet's confused.

"Because I love Zoe and so I have to be the one who saves her."

Janet looks at me with new respect in her eyes. I can tell she's proud of me.

"I really hope that your spell does the trick, but I have an idea. I'll talk to my uncle – he's the Chief of the Fire Department. I'll make sure he's on standby, just in case."

"Thanks Janet."

She beams at me. "Andy, you're going to be a hero."

Chapter Thirty Six

Supernatural Hero

I can't wait for tomorrow to come. I lie awake all night thinking about Zoe. About how I have to save her and her family. But what will happen if the whisper spell doesn't work?

I told Tom to be downstairs at 7 a.m. He's coming to get me on his new bike and we'll ride together to Zoe's. We'll go into her house and say the spell thirteen times, and then the evil spirit will disappear forever and the lives of Zoe and her family will be saved. But what will we say to her? She'll never believe us. She'll think we're out of our minds. And, anyway, if Zoe opens the door I'll probably choke and freeze or run away. I just can't let that happen again.

I hope Tom's spell is the real thing. If not, it's nerd city forever for me. If we save her and she knows it, maybe she'll give me one of Grandpa's famous second chances. I'd do anything to save her.

It's 6:32. I have to be downstairs in twenty-eight minutes. But where's Grandpa? He should be here. Maybe he's afraid? All I need is for someone to wake up now. I'd better get organized. I'll leave Mom a note so she won't worry. As I get my stuff together, I notice that I don't feel tired, but I'm shaking inside and I have that boiling volcano feeling again. Am I ready for battle? Am I going to be a hero?

I tear a page out of my notebook and write: "Already left for school – I start early today – I'll share Tom's lunch. Andy" I go to put the note on the fridge with a magnet and I see Grandpa sitting at the kitchen table, waiting for me.

"I came to be with you," Grandpa says and he smiles. "Today you're going to save Zoe."

"I sure hope so."

"Come on, you don't want to be late," Grandpa says.

I put the note in the middle of the fridge door and we go. The time is 6:54. We get into the elevator. Neither of us speaks. That's odd. Grandpa's hardly ever quiet. He should be giving me tons of advice. Is he scared? I look at him and he seems deep in thought. Tom's waiting for us at the entrance, with his new bike.

"Hi," I say. "You ready?"

"Ready to roll. Is Grandpa here?"

I look behind me and he's gone. I look all around, but I don't see him anywhere. I shake my head.

"We have to move," says Tom. And then I see Grandpa, sliding down an electric pole and making his way toward us, moving fast.

"Why did you disappear?" I ask.

"I went to talk to Grandma. I asked her to wish us luck," Grandpa says.

Tom hands me a helmet and I put it on and climb on the back of his bike. Grandpa sits on the handlebars. Tom switches on the electric motor and yells, "Let's go!" His voice sounds like the thunder of canons. Grandpa raises his arm to the sky and I feel like nothing can stop us and no one can stand in our way. The bike lurches forward and we're off. The time is 7:03 a.m. The wind is whipping my hair and the streets are practically empty. Grandpa is humming the theme music from an old cowboy movie.

As we approach Zoe's building, my body starts to shake and I'm having trouble breathing. I am so grateful to Tom. Without him I wouldn't get even this far. We stop at number eighteen and Tom locks his bike. It's 7:07 and I think I see Janet sitting in her car down the road, but I'm not sure. Tiny drops of sweat are beading on my forehead and the fear is wrapping around me like a blanket.. Grandpa is silent, standing on the side and watching Tom.

"Can you tell me the spell now?" I ask Tom.

"Remember, we have to say it thirteen times without stopping or else it won't work."

"What happens if we screw up?"

"No spirit can overcome the Whisper Spell," Tom assures me. "It's a secret spell that I found on King Solomon's seal." Tom reaches into his pocket, takes out a six-pointed star and hands it to me.

"This is King Solomon's seal," he says. "Keep it in your pocket and it will keep us safe. King Solomon used it for protection."

I put the star deep in my pocket and look over at Grandpa. He's giving me the thumbs up.

"How does the spell go?" I ask again.

"VOKKA, SORTINO, HOGAYA. Let's say it together: VOKKA, SORTINO, HOGAYA. Remember, thirteen times, without stopping."

All the way up in the elevator, I repeat the strange words to myself. At every floor I say them again and it feels like we're rising through a never-ending tower. VOKKA, SORTINO, HOGAYA, VOKKA, SORTINO, HOGAYA, until the elevator stops at the sixth floor. The time is 7:11. Outside the door we can hear the sounds of people moving around. I look at the door. The same sign hangs on it, only this time the letters seem to be dancing toward me. Everything's spinning around me. Grandpa's talking but I can't hear a word he's saying. It's as if I'm not even there.

Tom looks at me. "Now!" and he rings the bell. I hear someone coming and I pray it's not Zoe. I look down at my shoes.

"Hello!" I hear a voice. I look up and Zoe's mother Thelma is standing there.

"We came to talk to Zoe," I say.

"What's your name?" she asks.

"Andy," I say, wondering if she heard about the last time I stood in this spot.

Thelma smiles at me. "Come right in." Tom is the first to move and I follow. There's a strong smell of food cooking on the stove. Kind of unusual for so early in the morning, I think.

Grandpa's with us. Thelma goes to call Zoe. Then I notice a blurry image of a boy. He looks familiar, but I can't remember where I know him from. I look for Grandpa and I find him climbing up the wall and then I notice the huge black spirit. He's going after Grandpa.

"Watch out, Grandpa! He's here!" I scream.

Zoe comes running out of her room. She looks at me in amazement. "Andy, what are you doing here?"

The evil ghost turns away from Grandpa and focuses on me. I flatten myself against the wall. The ghost is moving toward me, holding a small flame.

Tom shouts, "Now!" We look at each other and at my signal we whisper fiercely, "VOKKA, SORTINO, HOGAYA!" The flame swells and Grandpa vanishes. The mantelpiece in the living room catches fire, orange and yellow flames licking at the wall, but Tom and I just keep chanting, "VOKKA, SORTINO, HOGAYA!"

Zoe and her mother stare at the fire. Zoe's dad comes out of the kitchen and runs for the door, holding her little sister. "What happened?"

All the while Tom and I are saying, "VOKKA, SORTINO, HOGAYA!"

Her mom grabs Zoe's arm and pulls her toward the door. For an instant our eyes lock. It's the first time we've ever looked at each other like that. She blinks, and I know it's a sign. Maybe I'm not a nerd anymore.

We're chanting it for the tenth time and I'm starting to get worried. The giant is howling and setting fire to the couch and the drapes. The room is filling with smoke and it's getting hard to breathe. I hear the sirens of the fire trucks in the distance. I know I have Janet to thank for that. The apartment is swirling with smoke, but I feel strong and when we say "VOKKA, SORTINO, HOGAYA!"for the twelfth time,

The spirit shrinks a little and he lets out a low groan. Out of the corner of my eye I see Zoe watching me from the doorway. She probably doesn't understand why I'm saying what I'm saying, but I think she knows I'm helping her.

As we whisper the spell for the thirteenth time, that evil spirit shrinks to a tiny dot. It floats out the window and vanishes. At that moment the firefighters burst through the door. While one of them escorts us into the hallway, the others spray the flames.

Tom and I look at each other and grin. We're both covered with soot.

"Everything okay?" I ask him.

"I told you it would work," he replies. We bump fists and do a little dance. I feel like shouting at the top of my voice.

Grandpa's holding both hands above his head like a champion. "You're a hero!" simply.

Tom and I walk toward the elevator. Zoe's standing there with her family and another fireman. She smiles at me—a dazzling perfect smile. I don't think I've ever felt so filled-up with happiness before. A part of me wonders if she understood what just happened, or does she think I'm some kind of weirdo for chanting like that? Either way, I happy knowing that I saved her and her family.

An older fireman comes up to me and tousles my hair and pats Tom on the back. "You boys are lucky," he says. "This isn't the first time there's been trouble at this address."

"What do you mean?" I ask him.

"I know this house. A little boy lived here once, but he was killed in a bicycle accident."

"What happened?"

"He was hit by a car and he wasn't wearing a helmet." The fireman shakes his head sadly. "It was a real tragedy."

"I think it was Victor," he says.

I feel as though my heart has stopped. I remember that blurry image. Now I'm sure. It was my Victor. My imaginary friend.

Chapter Thirty Seven

Zoe and Me

Mom drives me to school the next day and on the way she tells me that Janet called and told her she should be proud of me. "She said you're a real hero!" Mom smiles.

When the light turns red Mom looks at me. "Andy, I don't need anyone to remind me. I am always proud of you. You are a very impressive young man."

I feel like today is my big day, and then Mom adds, "And since your birthday's coming up, I want to have a party. Invite your whole class."

I can hardly believe my ears. She's never suggested that I have a party at home. She was probably afraid that no one would show up. But now I'm sure everyone will come. My smile almost splits my face in two. This time I'll celebrate like everyone else and invite everybody. I turn around to check out the back seat and Grandpa's right there.

"I told you we'd do it." He smiles.

"Thank you," I say.

Mom asks, "Is Grandpa here?"

"Yes, he's sitting in the back."

"Tell him that I love him and I miss him so much," she says. I see her eyes are shining with tears.

"Mom, Grandpa says to tell you that he loves you so much and he'll always be watching over us." Mom sobs but she's smiling too.

I get out at school. As usual as I walk through the entrance doors, my heart starts to pound. On the way to my class I pass by Sam, the old school janitor who died in a car crash last year. He says "Hi."

Grandpa asks who I'm talking to. I keep quiet.

Out the window I see Victor wearing a helmet as he rides his bike. He waves and shouts, "Helmets save lives!"

Then the first principal of the school walks past and nods to me. I've never met her, but I recognize her from all the graduating class photographs that are framed and hanging on the wall near the offices. I nod back.

"Who was that lady?" Grandpa asks. I don't answer but just keep walking to my class.

It's 8:52. I can't wait to see Zoe. Grandpa says, "Today you and Zoe will go to a movie."

"I don't think there will be any tickets left – it opens today," I say.

"I'm sure it will work out." Grandpa winks.

David comes out of the class and walks toward me. "Hey Andy, good job." I can't believe it. He's never talked to me like that before.

I look at Grandpa, but he's busy dancing on the ceiling.

David comes toward me again and I prepare myself for pain. He pats me on back.

"You're actually a hero," he adds.

I stop and look at him – he seems to be for real! I nod and rush to class. I want to see Zoe.

Everyone looks up when I walk in. For the first time ever I feel that they envy me; that they wish they were me.

I look over at Zoe's seat, but Sally's sitting there. My heart falls. I guess she didn't come to school today. There must be a lot of cleaning up to do at her house. Eyes down, I shuffle to my seat. And then I see Zoe – sitting in Sally's place, right next to mine. I've never been this close to Zoe. She's sitting there, smiling up at me. Our eyes meet. Grandpa's trying to attract my attention. He's pointing to the board. It takes me a minute to realize that everyone knows that I'm the kid who saved the Queen of the Class. The words on the board say: Andy saved me! Zoe.

The bell rings and the teacher walks in. Grandpa's doing a headstand on her desk. Zoe opens her backpack and takes out an envelope. She puts it on my desk.

"It's for you," she says. "You can open it."

I peel the top open and I find two tickets to the new 3D movie.

"Want to go to a movie with me?" Zoe asks.

"How did you know that…?"

Zoe leans over and whispers in my ear, "Your grandpa told me."

THE END

Time to say "thank you"

To my wife Revital: For the support and the sacrifice. You are my best listener, for hours at a time, always patient, supplying invaluable comments for every draft. You gave me excellent advice, sacrificed so many "husband hours," and were always there for me. You re-kindle my passion time and again and ignite my creative spark. Thank you for believing in me. I love you.

To my children: Lynn the enchantress, Donny the hero, and Hili the princess. I drove you crazy with my questions and you gave up so many "dad hours." You are my inspiration and contributed so many great ideas that helped me to realize the dream. I love you.

To Grandpa Binyamin: You passed on the writing bug. You are a huge source of inspiration. Thanks to you I saw the light…

To Grandpa Shlomo: You watch over me and show me the way from above.

To Grandpa Tata: You are my role model and a source of admiration. I lucked out.

To my family: You supported, taught and encouraged me at every opportunity. Words cannot express the gratitude I feel.

To my editor, Tsipi: You supported me all the way. I'm so glad I chose you. Thanks for unending support and encouragement. Thanks for your creative editing and insights and for believing in me. I am honored to be one of your writers.

To Inbal: You helped to keep me focused and on track. Without you I would never have met my deadlines. Your support and faith transformed the writing of my book into a total pleasure. Your dedication to the process is worthy of tremendous admiration.

To Gilah: Thank you for "getting" the book at first sight, for your dedication to the process and for transforming the book so that it can be read all over the world. Thanks for a brilliant translation, for your many insights, and for meeting our deadline. I am forever grateful.

To Yaniv: You helped me to hone the final product with tremendous enthusiasm and self-awareness. You give me strength to continue to fight for what I believe in. Thanks for your ongoing support and friendship.

To Silit: You were able to draw and give shape to my thoughts.

To David: You supported and encouraged me all the way – not something I take for granted.

To Adi: Thank you for the speed and the integrity

Special thanks to some nerds that inspired me:

Andy Murray-
"I was a geek" -You showed me that a geek can become a hero.

Bill Gates-
"If you don't like geeks you're in trouble".

Mark Zuckerberg-
"People assume that we're trying to be cool. That's never been my goal".

Maybe it's better to stay a nerd?

***

Please send reactions, comments, insights, complaints and
compliments to
erangadot@gmail.com
Find us on Facebook.com/supernaturalhero

CPSIA information can be obtained
at www.ICGtesting.com
Printed in the USA
LVHW01s0806280518
578667LV00009B/553/P